THE ISLE

B. BLACKWOOD

BRETAGEY PRESS

First Digital Edition: August 2023

Cover Designed by Shepard Originals

Edited by: Chrisandra Corrections

Fairy Proofmother Proofreading

Sisters Get Lit.erary

EAL Editing Services

❀ Created with Vellum

PROLOGUE

LAURA

This is the only way.

I clutch my phone tightly as I stare down at the screen. What should be a dull glow emanating from my screen is now beaming because of how dark the room is. Just the thought of what I am about to do weighs heavily on me. My hand trembles as I move to press record, finger hovering over the bright-red circle that will begin this voice memo. I need to make sure that each word is spoken clearly because it might be my last.

"My name is Laura Bennett." My words shatter the silence in the room, but remind me of the fear that feels as if it is seeping into my bones. "I live on Harrow Isle. I'm thirty-four, and my birthday is August twenty-eighth."

The facts tumble out of my mouth in a rush. The reality of what this means makes me even more emotional. I blink, forcing the tears away. "If you're listening to this voice memo, chances are... chances are that I'm no longer alive."

The confession forces a sob to fall from my lips before I

can catch it. I am proud of myself for managing to get those words out without crying. I debate with myself about stopping the recording so that I can pull myself together, but that is too much effort.

I need to focus. The only way this voice memo is going to get made is if I do it in one take.

I take a deep breath, trying to steady my voice, and continue speaking into the phone. "I'm so sorry for... everything."

I pause for a moment, my mind racing with memories of what I've been through. Things I don't want to, or have time to, relive. It is all too much.

"But I want to make this because I need to make sure the truth comes out." I take a deep breath in order to calm myself, but it doesn't matter. I am a lost cause, but I still press on. "If you're listening to this, please call Quinn Pierce. Her number is programmed into this phone. She'll know what to do next."

I pause the recording because of the tears streaming down my face. I play with the fabric of the red scarf that is draped on my shoulders. My security blanket of sorts, but it isn't doing anything to help me now.

Just before I get ready to speak, a flicker of movement in the periphery of my vision catches my attention. Panic slices through me almost immediately, and it is white hot and all-consuming.

The seconds tick by and I can't decide what to do. I am afraid to turn my head because I don't know what I will find.

"Who's there?" I demand, but my question doesn't hold much weight. My voice is shaky at best and the only weapon I have is my phone.

But luck is determined not to be on my side.

There is no response.

Dread fills me as I swallow hard, removing the lump from my throat. Reality decides it's time to slam into me once more because it is time for it to settle in.

I'm not alone.

1

QUINN

The rain drums a steady beat against the windowpane as I sit in my small, cozy office in Seattle. My office has always been my sanctuary amid the chaos, and I hope it provides the same for others. The walls are painted in calming shades of blue, creating a soothing atmosphere for my clients and me. A cream-colored sofa rests against one wall, piled with soft pillows of varying textures, something I'd thought to do to provide comfort during our sessions. Across from the sofa, two upholstered armchairs face each other. The setup is designed to encourage honest conversation and connection.

The scent of lemon hangs slightly in the air, something I put on to help wake me up. The aroma drifts from my oil diffuser on the corner shelf, nestled among an array of books and a potted plant whose purpose was to help bring life and energy to the room. My desk sits opposite the window, tidy and organized, fitting the aesthetic I thought I needed to portray.

The organization aspect is a work in progress at the

moment though because I can't find the business card of the restaurant I'm supposed to be going to later this week. The morning and afternoon have been a whirlwind of back-to-back sessions, and now with just over an hour break before the next client, I want to check out the restaurant. Frowning, I search through my desk drawer, looking for the card where I've booked a reservation.

Not finding it on my desk or in the drawers, I try to remember the last place I saw it. Then it hits me. I'd tucked it into my wallet for safekeeping.

Pulling out my leather wallet from my handbag, I flip through various compartments. As I'm searching, a small, worn photo peeks out from one of the folds.

It's an image I cherish, though not one I often share or talk about openly. The edges are soft from wear and tear, but the memory it has captured is perfectly vivid. My fingers brush over it, lingering for just a moment before putting it away. I'll look for the business card at another time.

I sigh as I turn back to my computer and begin typing away, figuring the best way to distract myself from my own thoughts would be to fill in my progress notes from the session before. My gaze drifts up temporarily and I see my diplomas and certificates hanging on the wall. Those are all worth it to be able to do what I love.

A light knock on the door drags my attention away from my computer. I'm not surprised to see Reese, my assistant, poking her head in.

"Quinn, I just forwarded something to you. Check your email," she says excitedly. "It's feedback from Mrs. Higgins. She just sent it in."

I turn back to my computer and find the email that Reese

forwarded me, curious about what has sparked her excitement. I scroll until I see the portion that Mrs. Higgins wrote and smile as I read her heartfelt words.

"Quinn's approach has transformed my life. Her kindness, empathy, and techniques have helped me break free from years of anxiety."

I look up from the email, meeting Reese's expectant gaze. "This is incredible, Reese. Thank you for bringing this to me."

"I was too excited and couldn't wait to show you. I'll let you get back to work because you have a client coming in about an hour."

I check the time before I go back to typing, determined to finish this progress report before my next client shows up. For some reason, the thought of not finishing it before she arrives bothers me, and I can't quite understand why.

Maybe it is because I've always prided myself on being able to understand and empathize with my clients' struggles. However, lately, I've been questioning whether I can truly help them heal when I'm still grappling with my own demons.

About an hour later, just as I'm pressing save on the file, there is a small knock on the door. I look over and say, "Come in."

Reese opens the door. "Your next client, Sarah Smith, has just arrived."

"Perfect, send her in."

As Reese leaves the doorway, I run my hands up and down my slacks. I hope that is enough to remove their clamminess.

"Ms. Pierce?"

The soft, tentative voice pulls me from my thoughts, and I look up to see Sarah standing hesitantly in the doorway.

"Hi, Sarah. Please call me Quinn. Come in and make yourself comfortable," I say, motioning to the armchairs across from me.

"Thank you," she says as she sits down in the chair closest to her. Her body language is guarded and unsure, and I don't blame her one bit. It's my job to provide her with a safe space to open up.

I lean forward, clasping my hands together, and offer her a reassuring smile. "Before we start, I want you to know that I'm here to listen to you. There's no judgment in this room."

She nods, but doesn't say a word. However, I do notice that she slightly relaxes a bit.

"Tell me what has brought you here today," I say gently.

"Um, well, I've been struggling with anxiety and depression for a while now, I think," Sarah admits.

I nod slowly. I empathize with her because it is a battle that I fight constantly. "It takes courage to seek help, Sarah. I want you to know that you're not alone in this journey."

"Sometimes I feel like I'm drowning," she confesses, and I can see the tears in her eyes. "It's like I can't breathe."

"Those feelings are valid, Sarah," I say as I reach over to grab a tissue from my desk to hand to her. I wait until she's finished wiping her eyes before I continue. "But together, we'll work on strategies to help you navigate all of this."

"Thank you, Quinn," she whispers.

We delve deeper into her experiences and emotions, and I do my best to help her as much as I can. With it only being her first session, I know it will take time for her to build up the systems that she needs to really use therapy as a tool to help her.

The hour comes to an end, and Sarah slowly stands up. She musters up a small smile and says, "Thank you for today."

I can't help but feel good because I'm helping her, even if it is by just being here and allowing her to talk. "Do you want to come see me again next week?"

"That would be great."

I give her an encouraging smile as I walk her out of my office and to Reese, who will be scheduling her next session.

As soon as I walk back into my office and close the door, my shoulders relax, and I take a few moments to sit still and reflect on my meeting with Sarah.

I jot down some notes from our session before packing up my things in preparation for heading home soon. After one final sweep of the office to make sure I haven't left anything behind, I grab my bag and walk out toward Reese's desk.

"You should go home."

She gives me a small smile. "I'm wrapping up a couple of things, but I'll be right behind you."

"Sounds good."

As I walk out of the office building, I take in a long, deep breath. Leaving my office and taking in the cool air is always invigorating. Not only that, but the knowledge that I have helped at least one person today makes everything worth it.

Especially when I couldn't help myself not that long ago.

The sun is beginning to set as I slip into my car, which is parked a short distance from my office. I can see that Seattle's rush hour is in full swing as a stream of headlights and taillights illuminates the busy streets. I join the traffic as the streetlights come to life, casting their soft, warm glow onto the sea of slowly moving cars. Despite the stop-and-start nature of city traffic, it gives me an opportunity to listen to a podcast while I'm traveling to and from work.

As I inch forward, I think about my clients' stories while trying to distance myself from the emotional weight of it all. This drive home is about attempting to leave my work at the office no matter how hard it actually is.

With the hum of the car engine and my podcast keeping me company, I steer through the traffic, and within forty minutes, I arrive safely at my home.

In the comfort of my own home, surrounded by all my things, the stress of the day starts to fade away. I take off the clothes I wore to work today and switch into a comfy loungewear set before making myself a cup of green tea. Once that is done, I sit down on my couch, and I finally allow myself to slowly unwind from everything that has happened today. I sip on tea and close my eyes for a moment, allowing the liquid to warm me from the inside out.

I jump slightly when my phone rings. I place my cup of tea on my coffee table and stand up to walk over to my bag.

Who the hell could be calling me right now?

I fish my phone out of the bag and find myself staring at my screen. My mouth drops open before I freeze. Laura Bennett's name is shining on my screen. Laura, my former college roommate who I am pretty sure I haven't talked to in, well, over a couple of years, is calling me?

Why is she calling me instead of sending a text message? And why now, after all this time? My thumbs hover over the phone, unsure of whether I want to answer the call or let it go to voice mail.

I swallow hard and I can't convince myself to pick up the phone. There's something off about this. Something I can't quite put my finger on.

The phone continues to ring, and I can almost swear it is echoing off the walls of my home. I have a choice to make and quick.

The pressure within me builds, and it still takes me another second to make a decision.

I finally answer the call.

2

QUINN

My voice shakes a little as I answer, "Hello, Laura?"

I hate that I am answering the phone this way, but there isn't anything I can do about it now.

"Quinn... it's Elliott."

Elliott. The name hits me like a freight train because I am not expecting his voice. He's Laura's husband, the man she dated on and off throughout college and married a couple of years ago. While I've met him a few times and attended their wedding, I don't know much about him, and I don't quite like the familiarity of his response.

"Uh, hi. Why are you calling me from Laura's phone? Where is she?"

"Quinn, I need your help," he says, and I can hear the strain in his voice.

I'm left with nothing but confusion. "Excuse me?"

"Laura is missing," the words flee his mouth in a hurry as if he doesn't have much of a choice, but to say it that quickly or else it will be lost forever.

My heart skips a beat as his words hit me like a sucker punch. That is the last thing I expected him to say. I understand what it means for someone to be missing, but my brain refuses to accept the connection that it is Laura we are talking about. What the hell happened?

"Quinn?" Elliott's voice interrupts my thoughts and brings me back to reality.

"Yes, yes, I'm here," I say as I'm still trying to wrap my mind around what he's telling me. I do care about Laura, but we haven't spoken in years. Why is he calling me, and why on Laura's phone? "Have the police been informed? What can I do to help?"

"Laura left her phone behind. I haven't given it to the police yet," he says, his voice cracking. I'm not sure what this has to do with anything, but I wait for him to continue. "While searching for her and trying to find clues to her whereabouts, I found a voice memo that said that I needed to contact you because you would know what to do. So, I hung on to it for you."

"But I don't know anything. Laura and I haven't spoken in a couple of years." If I remember correctly, we stopped speaking right after her wedding. There was no big argument or fight. Just two people who led busy lives that fell out of touch. I didn't know anything about how she'd been doing since they moved to the island.

"I'm relaying the information that I know and I'm not sure what else I should do."

"Okay," I say as I nod, even though Elliott can't see me. "Tell me everything you know. What happened the last time you saw Laura?"

Elliott takes a deep breath before he begins speaking

again. "She went missing about a week ago. The last thing we did together was have dinner. It was just a normal day. Mrs. Fleming prepared salmon and veggies for us, and we each had a glass of wine with dinner. We were laughing, talking about some silly article that someone wrote about her online. She seemed happy and everything seemed fine."

"Then what happened, Elliott?" I prompt, my voice gentle, and I recognize myself using the tone of voice I use with my clients during a session.

"We grabbed our dishes and brought them to the sink. After we were done, she said she was going to go up to her office," Elliott continues. "She often did that after dinner, so it wasn't out of the ordinary. She liked to read a few emails to wind down and kill time before bed. She kissed me goodbye and went upstairs."

"Did you check on her at all when she was in her office?"

"No. I did walk past her office at some point and the door was closed. I try not to disturb her and sometimes she falls asleep in there too, so it isn't unusual for me to end up not seeing her until the next morning."

"What was she wearing the last time you saw her?"

"A white T-shirt, a pair of jeans, and her red scarf. She was barefoot while she was eating dinner and when she went upstairs, and I didn't notice any of her shoes missing either. Police have already come and couldn't find anything that would indicate foul play. She was gone."

I knew the exact scarf he was talking about. It had been something Laura's grandmother had given her before she passed away. She'd worn it off and on throughout college, especially when she'd had a big exam or project that she wanted to do well on. She told me once that she wanted her grandmother to be with her during those times and having the scarf was her way of achieving that.

I put the phone on speaker and set it back down on my counter. It gives me the opportunity to rub my hands across my face as I try to figure out what to do or say next. I don't know what to do, but I can't just let my old friend be in danger and do nothing about it. "How can I help?"

"Would you come to Harrow Isle? I know it would be a lot for you to pick up things last minute."

"It's not a problem at all. I will do it for Laura and to do my part in making sure that she gets home safely."

"Thank you, Quinn. All I can say is thank you."

"Of course."

Elliott clears his throat and says, "I'll handle your travel arrangements and anything you need while you're here. I'll send a text message once I have everything squared away."

"Thank you. And we'll find her, Elliott. I promise."

"Goodbye."

With that, I hang up the phone and give myself the opportunity to process what I've just learned and what I've committed myself to. I know what it is like to have someone you love go missing. The torment that it inflicts on a person is indescribable. The emotions that course through a person as you try to navigate your new normal causes what feels like a version of whiplash. This is just one of the many reasons that I need to do this.

With my decision made, I grab my laptop from my workbag, determined to find whatever I can about Laura's disappearance. Elliott didn't mention any media attention, but if she's missing, shouldn't there be at least local reports about her disappearance?

I click on my web browser and immediately start typing Laura's name into the search engine. I can feel my pulse racing as I scour news articles and social media posts for any clues that might help me understand what happened to Laura. I shake my head as I reach dead end after dead end, and again when it hits me that there is practically nothing about her disappearance. It's as if she vanished without a trace, which doesn't make sense.

I stare at a current picture of Laura. Her shoulder-length blonde hair has subtle highlights. She is made up perfectly and standing next to her is Elliott. Together they look like the quintessential couple who lives a perfect life. Hell, they even left their perfect lives in New York City to move to Harrow Isle, and the only reason why I know that is because I'd seen it mentioned on social media about a year ago.

As I scroll through her posts, each paints a picture of the perfect life that Laura has curated. Among the photos, I find one that sends a jolt of confusion through me.

There is a photo of Laura and another woman, both with windswept hair, standing on what looks like cliffs. Their smiles are broad, their faces close in what seems like a candid moment of shared laughter. But it's the caption below it that makes me do a double take, *Exploring Harrow Isle, with my lovely new friend, Joanna. Can't believe we've only just met!*

What is becoming clear to me is that the Laura Bennett I knew is very different from the Laura Bennett she is today. Not that that is surprising given that we'd known each other in our late teens and early twenties and now we are both in our thirties. Years have passed since the last time we saw each other, and none of these photos show the infectious laughter that I knew she had. But there is something in the photos I'm looking at that is slightly unsettling to me.

She is smiling in the photos, but the happiness doesn't reach her eyes. Her gaze almost appears to be lifeless.

It reminds me of how my photos looked about five to six years ago.

But I can't focus on myself right now. I shake away the unsettling familiarity that I notice between us, which sends a shiver down my spine and reminds me of the urgency of the situation. What I need to focus on is the fact that she is missing and every passing second matters.

"Where are you, Laura?" I whisper, but of course Laura doesn't respond. The only answer I receive back is silence.

3

QUINN

A couple of days later, I somehow manage to tie my hair in a ponytail even though it is whipping across my face. It is a bit of a foolish attempt because strands of my hair still manage to get out and go back to slapping me in the face.

But I am here.

The boat's engine hums, sending soft vibrations through the deck as we ride through the water. The light fog that is all around us creates a haunted feeling, already giving me bad thoughts about this place. I tighten the grip I already have on my cross-body bag and scan my environment. Nothing surrounds us but water and I am beginning to wonder if we are even going in the right direction.

Elliott did everything in his power to make sure I made it to Harrow Isle safely. That included chartering a private plane for me and then having me driven to the port, where I was able to catch this private boat.

I close my eyes for a moment, and I swear I can almost taste the sea air on my lips. The gray sky above seems to mirror the waters beneath and the storm churning within me. It is as if Mother Nature herself is warning me of the things I'm going to find when I reach my destination. I watch as what I can only assume is the silhouette of Harrow Isle emerges from the thin fog, and my heart slams in my chest.

As we get closer, the rugged shoreline becomes clearer. I can see a lighthouse and what I think are houses and businesses, but the state of the buildings I see does little to ease the unsettled feeling that is sitting in my gut. The more details I'm able to make out, the more one thing becomes apparent.

We are almost there.

"We're coming up on our destination," the boatman says before he lets out a loud grunt. When we are within feet of the shore, he lessens the throttle of the engine. He points toward the island's rocky shore. "You sure you want to be dropped off here? There's still time for me to take you back."

"Positive," I reply without looking at him.

Nothing but the sounds of the boat and the water around us can be heard for several minutes as we make our way to the shore. He doesn't say a word as he ties the boat, but when I think he's about to turn around and help me off, he speaks. "There's no way I can convince you to let me take you back so you can hop on a plane and get the hell away from this place?"

That forces me to direct my attention fully to the man standing next to me. "No. I'm here to make sure that a friend of mine is okay."

The boatman shrugs and doesn't say another word. His silence only brings more unsettling feelings to me as I try not to show that I'm having second thoughts about all this too.

When the vessel is secure, he makes sure the boat isn't going to move before helping me step out of the boat, followed by my bags.

"Do you have someone picking you up?"

I nod. "Yes, he should be here any second." Just as the words leave my lips, a black sedan that looks to be in perfect condition from here drives toward the marina, and based on its description, I assume that it is Elliott. "I think that's my ride."

"You just lost your opportunity to get the fuck out of here," he says, mostly under his breath. He turns back to the boat but pauses temporarily and then says, much louder, "Just remember outsiders aren't really welcome on Harrow Isle. Be careful."

I stare at him for a moment, not sure what to say in response. I wait a beat before I reply. "Thanks for the warning," I say just before he starts the boat once more.

I find myself watching as the boat drifts away, soon to be swallowed by the fog. He leaves like his ass is on fire. The visual makes me shake my head, given how close I am to the water. I turn to face the island, not sure what the hell I'm about to get myself into.

When the car parks in front of me, I recognize the man sitting in the driver's seat immediately.

Elliott Bennett.

He pops the trunk of his car and then gets out. As he stands up, I can't help but notice the streaks of silver that line his dark hair. It is easy to see, based on the look in his eyes, that he didn't get much sleep last night. The stress is written all over his face, and understandably so.

"Quinn." His voice is tense, and I hope that my being here

will allow him to share the burden of this traumatic event. I can't take the pain away, but I can do my best to try and find her, especially if Laura requested my presence.

"Yes, it's great to see you again, Elliott. Wish it wasn't under such terrible circumstances," I manage to say as Elliott walks toward me.

"Same," he says as his gaze locks on mine. "I'm glad you were able to come on such short notice."

"I shifted a lot of my schedule, but there was no way I wasn't coming. I want to help find Laura."

"I appreciate it more than you know. Let's get your things in the car and then we can head to my home," he says.

I nod. He takes my bags from me and puts them in the trunk before opening the passenger door for me. I slide into the seat, relieved that I finally made it here.

Once we are situated in the car, Elliott pulls out of the marina parking lot. His hands clench tightly onto the steering wheel as he stares straight ahead while navigating his way through the fog that covers Harrow Isle. The farther away we move from the docks, I find myself looking around at the island as I try to get a small feel for the community.

A sense of unease wins out as I can't shake the idea that I shouldn't be here.

But the man that brought me here by boat was right. By not leaving with him, I missed my opportunity to leave the island. Is this a trap? Did I make a foolish mistake?

No, something is wrong, and Laura is missing. That is what I need to focus on. Bringing Laura back home.

My attention is drawn back to the drive. The fog grows thicker around us, creating an almost claustrophobic atmosphere that I want to crawl out of. The journey is silent except for a few areas that Elliott points out to help me get familiar with the town and to point out some of Laura's favorite places.

Harrow Isle's landscape reveals itself in glimpses, the branches of leafless trees that paint a creepy picture, the abandoned homes and businesses that now have over-grown lawns and run-down buildings. From what I can see, it almost feels as if this place is frozen in time, and the scenery that surrounds me does nothing to shake the unsettling feeling that has made its home in my body.

I turn to Elliott and am slightly startled by what I find. His entire presence is mechanical to me. It is as if a robot is in the car with me instead of a human being. He's focused completely on the road ahead, but there is more tension in his shoulders than I noticed when we first got in the car.

I look out the window, reminding myself it's rude to stare at someone like this. It isn't until he clears his throat, breaking the silence between us, that I turn my head to look back at him. But he doesn't look at me.

"Harrow Isle can be interesting," he says, his voice rougher than I remember from our brief phone conversation just a couple of days ago.

I glance sideways at him, attempting to make sense of him and what he is talking about. I'm drawn back to the boatman who brought me here and his plea that I reconsider staying here. "What do you mean *interesting*?"

He doesn't say a word as he turns onto a narrow road which is decorated with even more trees that have lost their leaves. My entire experience on this island so far is creepy, including the man I am sitting next to. It is strange because the few times we'd been around each other when Laura was present hadn't given me these vibes.

"You're already experiencing the change in weather. A few hours ago, the sun was shining, for instance."

"What a wonderful welcome," I mutter under my breath.

Elliott doesn't indicate that he heard me. Instead, he focuses on turning down another narrow street and it takes me longer than it would normally to read a faded sign that says Bennett Estate.

"Is there anything else?"

"There's one other thing." He pauses, and as I wait for him to finish the rest of his statement, I watch as the Bennett mansion comes into view.

The home stands tall and imposing, a relic of a different time, yet because of what I've seen of Harrow Isle, it fits in perfectly. If I had to describe its architecture, I would say it leans more Gothic in nature, and because of the fog and overcast skies, the building looks even more haunting. The tall windows and vines that crawl up its walls fit the aesthetic to a tee. If someone were to tell me that no one is living here, I would believe them even with the smoke I see rising from the chimney.

The Laura I knew back in college would have been leery about stepping foot on these grounds, let alone living in this house.

"There are some superstitions that you should be aware of."

Elliott's words make my brain short-circuit temporarily. It takes me a second to find the words to say the question on the tip of my tongue. "What type of superstitions?"

"The locals believe a bunch of things, including some

things about my home. Stories about my ancestors and events that happened here. The house, to some, is considered to be... tainted, for lack of a better word. However, Laura and I never thought anything of those stories."

I blink slowly, allowing myself to digest his words. I shift my gaze to look back at the house in front of me as Elliott slows the car down.

He throws the car into park but doesn't immediately get out of the vehicle. For what feels like the first time, he turns to face me, looking me directly in the eyes. "No matter what you do in order to help me find Laura, I do ask that you be careful. Respect this house, respect the island and its ways. Even if you don't believe the same things the locals do, it's best you don't show that you don't. Trust me."

4

QUINN

As I step out of the vehicle, I get a better look at the slightly crumbling façade of the mansion. Elliott walks up to the front door, and it opens before he can lift a finger.

As I walk into the home, a line of people are standing near the entrance. We are greeted by the long-serving staff of the mansion, each wearing a crisp uniform. I immediately notice that their expressions show nothing but curiosity and caution toward me, the newcomer. They exchange glances with one another before offering hesitant smiles.

"Ms. Pierce," a woman who looks to be in her sixties with silver hair greets me. "I am Mrs. Annette Fleming, Mr. Bennett's housekeeper. We've been expecting you."

"Hello, Mrs. Fleming," I say, extending a hand. She hesitates, then shakes it briefly before withdrawing.

"Your room has been prepared," she informs me, her gaze flicking from me to Elliott and back again. "If you need anything, please don't hesitate to ask. Mr. Gregory will be taking your bags up to your room. I'll show you where it is."

As if on cue, a man with slightly stooped shoulders walks past us. His suit, though it seems of good quality, doesn't quite fit him right. The sleeves are a little too long, and the pants a tad too short. His thinning hair is a somewhat unkempt mix of brown and gray, giving the impression he attempted to comb it, but it might have gotten messy throughout the day. On his face, he sports a pair of thick glasses that magnify his eyes that seem to dart all over the place.

As Mr. Gregory leaves the home, I turn, and watch Elliott leave as well. I'd been expecting him to give me a tour of his home, but with him going, it is clear that he has no problem leaving me alone in a room full of people I don't know. It's an interesting choice, especially when I'm trying to help him find his wife.

"Thank you." I nod as I turn my attention back to Mrs. Fleming.

She then starts up the stairs and I follow, allowing her to lead me farther into this dark, gloomy mansion. I spare a look over my shoulder and watch as the other staff members linger in the shadows, still watching me with a mix of curiosity and wariness. Their body language speaks volumes. It's easy for me to tell that they are unsure of my presence, and to be honest, I don't blame them.

The eerie silence of the mansion continues as I follow Mrs. Fleming down a long, dimly lit hallway. With each step I take, I can't help but wonder if I've made the right choice by deciding to stay here instead of getting a room somewhere in town.

Mrs. Fleming points out a few rooms to me, including

Laura's office. "Your room is just up ahead," she says softly as we continue to walk. She finally pauses in front of a door, grabs the doorknob, and pushes it open, revealing a spacious, yet somber bedroom.

"Thanks again," I say, stepping inside and surveying my surroundings. The room isn't terrible by any stretch of the imagination, and I'm happy to say that my assumptions about the room based on what I saw of the mansion's exterior, and the foyer were wrong.

The walls are a soft gray and against one of them stands a huge four-poster bed. Large windows are framed by heavy velvet drapes. I glance outside, but can't see much due to the fog that still hangs heavily in the air. There is a fire in the fireplace, slightly warming the chill that is present throughout the home.

An older-looking writing desk, a small couch, and a pair of decorative chairs are placed around the room. There's a dresser in the corner with a mirror above it, finishing off the major furniture pieces in the room. For being a guest room, I'm surprised by its size, but I don't let Mrs. Fleming in on the thoughts crowding my brain.

"Is everything to your liking?" Mrs. Fleming asks as she folds her hands in front of her.

I nod, not trusting my voice in this unsettling ambience.

"Good. Your bathroom is right through that door and your closet is just over there. Mr. Bennett would like to see you in his office when you're ready. It's downstairs, the first door on the left if you're walking in from the front door," she informs me before turning to leave.

Mr. Gregory appears with my bags and leaves them near

the dresser without saying a word. Both of them walk out into
the hallway, with Mrs. Fleming grabbing the doorknob once
more. With a soft click, the door closes behind her and I'm
left alone.

I take a few moments to settle in and unpack my things. I
move around the room, sorting out my items. Once I am
done, I take a deep breath and quickly make my way
downstairs.

The hallway is still silent as I walk through it, keeping my
steps light as if I'm afraid to disturb anyone else that might be
around. Why I'm acting this way when it's still the middle of
the day is anyone's guess, but for some reason, I feel the need
to do so. Finally, I'm standing outside Elliott's office door and
take another deep breath before raising my hand to knock
lightly against the wood. The sound echoes slightly, but it
does its job, and I hear a muffled response from inside before
being given permission to enter.

As I step into Elliott's office, I notice that the walls have
dark mahogany panels on them, and a huge desk sits in the
middle of the room. He rises from his chair and pulls something out of a drawer. It takes me only a second to realize that
it's a phone. I assume it's Laura's phone which he used to
contact me.

"I figured you would want to get started right away, so
here's Laura's phone with all of the voice memos she left
on it."

"Have you listened to them?"

He shrugs. "A few, but there were so many and a lot of it
seemed like rambling. I couldn't put together where she
might be from them."

His indifference is slightly alarming. "Were there any other messages? Notes?"

He hesitates a moment before replying, "No, but she always retreated to her office when she wanted solitude or was working on something personal."

I remembered him saying that and it was the next place I was going to go.

"Have you talked to the police?" I ask.

Elliott runs a hand through his hair, releasing a weighty sigh. "Sheriff Murray is aware and is doing his best, but outside of the voice memo, there's no sign of foul play. I'm trying to work with the proper authorities and bring in help, but the red tape is something else. The voice memo she left was what really kicked all this off."

I raise an eyebrow at him. "What did that voice memo say?"

"I'll play it for you."

He reaches across his desk, taps on Laura's phone, and then turns it so the speaker faces both of us. A familiar voice fills the room. It's Laura.

"My name is Laura Bennett. I live on Harrow Isle. I'm thirty-four, and my birthday is August twenty-eighth." She hesitates, her voice breaking. "If you're listening to this voice memo, chances are... chances are that I'm no longer alive."

She takes a deep breath and then says, "I'm so sorry for... everything."

Elliott and I share a look before I glance back down at the phone.

"But I want to make this because I need to make sure the truth comes out." Laura takes a deep breath once again. "If you're listening to this, please call Quinn Pierce. Her number is programmed into this phone. She'll know what to do next."

The recording ends abruptly and I'm left speechless. I continue to stare at the phone, hoping that Laura's voice will start again, but it doesn't.

I look up at Elliott and say, "I might not know her as well as I used to, but I have a hard time believing that she would just leave. At least not without saying something."

His eyes meet mine and he says, "I agree. I know it's been years since you two spoke, but after her voice memo mentioned you, I couldn't not ask you to come. I'm desperate."

"Can I have her phone? To listen to the other voice memos?"

All Elliott does is nod and I reach for the device. A sinking feeling settles in my stomach.

"I hope this is enough to get you started. Let me know if you have any questions. Also, if you want to explore her office, feel free. Sheriff Murray and his team have already come and gone," Elliott says, effectively dismissing me.

I turn on my heel and begin to walk to the door when I hear Elliott's voice once more.

"Oh, and Quinn," he adds, and I turn around to look at him. "Mrs. Fleming and Mr. Gregory have already been informed of this, but if you need a car, any time, they'll make sure it's available for you. If you need anything else, we'll make sure you have that as well. I'll spare no expense to have Laura back."

With a small nod, I turn around and walk toward the office door. I want to do anything to help my friend, but all of this is weighing heavily on me.

Hell, is Laura even alive?

The question swirls around me as I leave Elliott's office, closing the door behind me and walking back up the stairs to Laura's private sanctuary.

5

QUINN

The door creaks as I push it open, stepping into Laura's private office. It is as if the air has been holding its breath since Laura went missing. The furnishings here are brighter in color, much different from what I've seen in the rest of the house.

The first thing that strikes me is the amount of natural light that would be in this room. A large bay window would offer a breathtaking view of what I assume to be the rugged coastline I noticed just as I arrived on the island. Sleek, light-colored wooden furniture fills the room, well balanced with the room's off-white walls.

I take my time, allowing my eyes to scan the room, choosing to linger on Laura's personal belongings. I can't help but feel like an intruder in this space, but if it provides a clue as to what happened here, then so be it.

I take inventory of the different types of books on her shelf before I stop suddenly. My attention is caught by a framed photograph on her bookshelf of Laura and me, taken during our college years. Our arms are entwined, joy can clearly be seen on our faces. We are standing in front of our college library after just having left there after studying. I reach out and allow my fingers to trace the edge of the frame. My eyes are glued to the red scarf that was such a fixture of hers back then.

I pick up the frame and I remember that afternoon. We'd both had our morning classes canceled and we'd spent a couple of hours in the library before walking out to enjoy the afternoon sun. I'm not one to miss college much, but the fondness of the memory has me longing to go back there.

I put the photo back in its place and look down at Laura's phone in my hand. I scroll down until I find the first memo on her phone, hoping that going in chronological order might provide a clue that somehow everyone else missed. This voice memo is from just over a year ago.

The sound of a soft sigh starts the recording. "It's one of those days where Harrow Isle feels both familiar and foreign. Years coming here and still every now and then, something happens that catches me off guard."

The recording continues with a few seconds of silence followed by an audible deep inhale. "Okay, first voice memo. Not sure why I'm doing this, but hey, why not? What do I have to lose? This is the start of a new beginning, right? This can be a way to keep track of my thoughts, I guess. An audio diary, if you will."

There's a soft chuckle. "Moved to Harrow Isle today. It's very different than living in New York City, that's for sure. Being back in Elliott's hometown is exciting, and I'm okay with admitting that he was right. Harrow Isle would be a great place for us to settle down and start a family. Everyone seems to know everyone, and I feel like a bit of an outsider, but I'm sure with time, people will be more welcoming."

Another small sigh and then, "The first thing I unpacked was my grandmother's scarf and immediately threw it on. Funny how an object can calm you down, and I'm grateful to still have it. I definitely needed it today because the whole day has been... overwhelming, to say the least."

A loud creak can be heard faintly in the background and the recording ends with a soft click. I debate whether it's worth me starting another one of Laura's voice memos when a knock sounds on the door. I nearly jump out of my skin as I spin around to see who it is.

It's Mr. Gregory standing in the doorway. "Ms. Pierce, dinner is ready."

"Thank you," I reply hesitantly, still reeling from the abrupt interruption. How long has he been standing there? And how could I not have heard him?

I stuff Laura's phone in my back pocket and follow the man out of the room, down the stairs, and into the dining room.

A long mahogany table stretches across the floor, and I find myself thinking it looks like a dark river sitting in the center of the room. Its surface gleams beneath the light shining down from the chandelier. Fine china pieces are arranged at the two place settings, and candles sit in the middle of the table, flickering off the surface of the plates.

A feast awaits us as a bunch of dishes are laid out all over the table. The smells of the food fill the room, and I can see roast beef, buttery garlic potatoes, string beans, and freshly baked bread that all look delicious. But even as my stomach growls with hunger, I find it difficult to focus on the meal. My mind is consumed by thoughts of Laura and how she is doing.

"Quinn, help yourself to the food here. If you want something different, my staff can whip something else up."

I look over and find Elliott standing in another doorway opposite the one I entered. I glance at him, trying to read the emotions that he is trying to keep hidden. Based on what I can see and given the tone of his voice, I can tell that he was slightly more welcoming when I arrived, but now it seems as if the man before me has closed himself off, and I can't help but wonder why.

"Thank you," I say, almost under my breath, before I reach for the serving utensils and fill my plate with the tempting dishes. I sit down and begin to eat once Elliott gathers his own food.

Elliott's distant demeanor becomes more apparent as the meal continues. His shoulders are stiff, his posture rigid, and he refuses to hold a conversation or look in my general direction.

"Is everything alright, Elliott?" I ask in hopes of breaking the silence.

He blinks several times as if he had been in a faraway land and has only just come back to his dining room table. "Yes, just preoccupied with thoughts of Laura."

I nod, understanding that completely. Having your spouse missing would be enough to have anyone be out of it. I watch as Elliott reaches for his wineglass.

"Has anyone said anything else about Laura's disappearance since I left your office?" I ask, hoping that I might have more to go on.

Elliott tenses more, his fingers tightening around the stem of his wineglass. "No," he says curtly. "Not a word."

I expect him to ask about what I found, but to my surprise, he doesn't bother.

As I open my mouth to say something, the whole room goes black, plunging us into darkness without warning. The suddenness of the event has me feeling disoriented and my heart pounds in my chest.

"Wh—what the hell just happened?" I finally get out, trying to scan my surroundings in the now-limited light we have. I'm thankful for the candles that are set on the table.

"Power outage," Elliott replies. "Not uncommon on Harrow Isle, unfortunately. I'll go check the fuse box."

His chair scrapes against the wooden floor, his footsteps leave the room, and I'm alone in the darkness. My mind races as I think of a million and one different scenarios for why we lost power and none of them make me feel rosy on the inside.

Where is his staff? I didn't hear anyone leave the house, so why didn't they come in to check on their employer?

As I'm about to pull out my phone or Laura's to use as a flashlight, I jump when I see something out of the corner of my eye. I turn my head more to get a better look, but I see nothing. I didn't get a good enough look to tell me exactly what it was, but I know I don't like it.

I start to stand up, trying to convince myself that it is my imagination playing tricks on me. However, I don't really want to wait around to ensure the image is only a fabrication of my mind.

Pushing down the panic, I decide to shake off the paranoia, and I manage to grab my phone. It is probably just the vibes I've been feeling ever since I arrived getting to me. I turn on the flashlight function of my phone and walk out of the room. I have no idea what is taking Elliott so long, but I have no intention of waiting here to find out.

I leave the dining room and head toward the stairs. My heart is slamming in my chest as I make my way up. All the while, I keep glancing around, expecting to see something that will confirm whether this whole thing is just a figment of my imagination. But it's all quiet. It's just me and the shadows that surround me.

Finally, I reach the top of the stairs and think, *screw it*. I make a beeline for the guest room door. Throwing it open, I quickly shut it behind me, sliding the lock into place before exhaling in relief at being safe in my own space.

As I walk to the bed I will be sleeping in tonight, the lights suddenly turn back on, and I could cry. But when I look at the nightstand closest to the window, I almost scream.

Sitting there is the photo of Laura and me from her office, staring back at me.

6

QUINN

The last thing I remember looking at while I'm awake is the picture of Laura and me, but as soon as I close my eyes it morphs into a shoreline I don't recognize. The sun is high in the sky, and everything feels peaceful.

Somewhere in the distance, children's laughter can be heard and it's the most pure and innocent sound that I've ever heard. Drawn to it, my eyes land on a young girl building a sandcastle near the shore.

Out of nowhere, the serenity of the beach transforms. Its soft sands change into the rocky terrain of Harrow Isle. The waves, once calm, are now wild.

Suddenly, Laura sits down next to the little girl. She looks at the girl whose face I can't see. A silent understanding passes between them as they begin to walk away from the water. My heart races, urging them to move faster, to escape.

I try to scream, to shout a warning to them, but nothing happens. I can only watch them.

Suddenly my eyes snap open and I take several deep

breaths to calm down. I watch as the morning light creeps through the gaps in the heavy curtains. I can't help but think it is ironic that the stream of light is casting a warm glow on the photograph of Laura and me.

As I lie in bed, my thoughts drift back to last night's awkward dinner, the power going out and then the dream I just awoke from. Something is wrong here, and I'm willing to bet money whatever it is has something to do with Laura's disappearance. While that doesn't explain my dream, all of the things that are going on are getting to me.

I drag myself out of bed. The cool wooden floor sends a small shiver up my legs as I pad across the room to the en suite bathroom. Steam fills the air as I turn on the water and then step into the shower, letting the hot water wash away my sleepiness. I watch as the water circles the drain before I catch myself in the light daydream I've fallen into.

After drying my body off and dressing in warm attire, I grab my phone, Laura's phone, and the picture frame before I leave the guest room and walk downstairs. I've only listened to a couple of the memos, and I need to listen to the rest. It has been difficult for me to listen to them all because of how many there are.

The aroma of freshly brewed coffee fills the air as I enter the dining room, where Mrs. Fleming is arranging an assortment of breakfast items on the table.

"Good morning," I say as I stroll past Mrs. Fleming. She gives me a tight smile and I wonder what that is all about.

"Good morning, Ms. Pierce," she replies. "I trust you slept well?"

Her question seems awfully presumptuous given the circumstances and the state of this home, but I don't voice my thoughts. "About as well as could be expected," I offer, my fingers brushing against the frame in my hand.

"Please have a seat," she says, gesturing toward the chair that is in front of the table setting. The rest of the table, outside of the food, is bare.

"Thank you," I reply, taking the seat. My gaze drifts over the table once more before I ask, "Mrs. Fleming, where is Elliott?"

"Mr. Bennett had some urgent business to attend to," she answers, avoiding eye contact. Her vague response raises a red flag, but I decide not to press further for now.

"Ah, okay," I say as I take a cup and pour myself some coffee. After making it to my liking, I take a sip, enjoying the sensation that courses through me. It's the only time I've felt relief while being here and it's fleeting. I take a deep breath and steel myself for the questions I need to ask. "Mrs. Fleming, could you tell me more about Laura's disappearance?"

"One evening, she was here, and the next morning she was gone," she replies, her voice cracking slightly. "It's been difficult for everyone."

"Did Laura have any enemies on the island?" I ask, hoping not to upset her.

"Enemies?" Mrs. Fleming repeats, her brow furrowing. "No, Laura was well liked by everyone here. She was always so kind and generous." She hesitates for a moment but doesn't elaborate.

I nod slowly, mulling over her response. Mrs. Fleming's response differed from the memo that Laura left, but a lot could change in the years that she'd been here. I can't help but think that Mrs. Fleming is holding something back. I swallow my suspicion for now, but I still have more questions.

I glance at the picture frame again before showing it to Mrs. Fleming. "This photo appeared in my room last night. Do you have any idea how it got there?"

Mrs. Fleming looks taken aback as she walks over and studies the image, her eyes widening with surprise. "I—I don't know. Perhaps one of the staff placed it there by mistake."

"If you know something about this, please tell me." I don't hide the fact that I am dying to know how it ended up there and why.

She meets my gaze for a moment before quickly looking away. "I'm sorry, Ms. Pierce," she says, avoiding my eyes. "I truly don't know how it ended up there. If you need anything else, I'll be in the kitchen."

I wait until she leaves before I turn to eat my breakfast in silence.

Once I'm done, Mrs. Fleming returns, this time with a slight smile. "Is there anything else you need before you start your day?"

"Actually," I say, taking a deep breath. "I was hoping to explore Harrow Isle today. I feel like I need some fresh air."

"Of course," she says, her expression unreadable. "I'll arrange for a car to be brought around for you. Should be ready to go in ten minutes."

"Thank you, Mrs. Fleming." I offer her a smile, hoping to show that she can trust me, but her expression remains unchanged. I push my seat back and return to the guest bedroom to make sure I have everything I need in the bag I will be bringing with me today.

When I return downstairs, Mr. Gregory is waiting for me

by the front door, keys in hand. He doesn't say a word, just hands the keys to me.

"Thank you, Mr. Gregory," I reply, accepting the keys happily. When he doesn't give me a response, I give him a small head nod and walk past him. I step outside and quickly notice that the fog has lifted even though it is still overcast. I approach what looks to be a brand new, navy-blue sedan, and once I'm seated behind the wheel, I let out a sigh of relief. *I'm free... somewhat.*

In the passenger seat, I find a map and a set of locations with their addresses on another piece of paper. I start tracing the lines of streets and landmarks as I plan my route. *Thank you, Mr. Gregory.*

Instead of using the map, I plug the address of a local coffee shop into my phone, and I start the car. The engine purrs softly as I navigate the narrow driveway of the Bennett estate. As I drive into town, using the GPS to guide me, I notice some charming touches mixed in with old-fashioned and modern architecture.

Once I'm near the coffee shop, I park the car on a side street and step out of the vehicle. The first thing I'm hit with is the crisp sea air. My eyes are drawn to the town square at the heart of it all, with its food market and friendly chatter among the locals. I decide to start my investigation there instead of the coffee shop. Here's to hoping I pick up any useful information about Laura. Then I can head to my original destination.

As I wander through the square, I overhear snippets of conversation. Some of it is mundane, including complaints about the weather or talking about their children, but other tidbits catch my attention.

"Did you hear about the woman who is now staying at the Bennett estate?" one woman whispers to another. "Isn't that odd, given that Laura is missing?"

"Another woman?" her friend replies, raising an eyebrow. "What's she doing there? Is Elliott already moving on from his wife? Wouldn't be unheard of in that family, honestly."

Apparently my arrival on the island has not gone unnoticed, and I can't help but feel like an unwelcome outsider. It brings up Laura's oldest voice memo once more.

I step into an interesting little shop that seems to specialize in antiques, its walls covered in dusty shelves filled with odd trinkets. A bell above the door announces that I'm entering. I'm greeted by the store owner, Angela, who is a middle-aged woman with silver-streaked hair, and I can see that she is hesitant to talk to me. I wonder if this will hit the gossip mill as soon as I leave the shop.

"You're new here," she states matter-of-factly. "Can I help you with something?"

It's easy for me to hear the mistrust in her voice.

"I'm just exploring," I reply, but I hold back. I don't want to divulge too many details about my true purpose on Harrow Isle. "I was hoping to learn more about the history of the island and the people who live here."

She gives me a curt nod and gestures to a few things. "Every item here has a story to tell."

I look around at several things, and I manage to get her to share with me tidbits of the history of Harrow Isle and its prominent families. She names the Bennetts, and I'm not surprised about that, but when she says the Hartleys, I give her a confused look. Who are they?

"Luke Hartley owns the only bar in town, The Harbor's

Edge. His family's been here since the founding of the island as well."

So the Bennetts and the Hartleys have been here for generations. An interesting fact, and it makes sense, given what I've seen of the Bennett mansion. "Thank you for talking with me," I say, genuinely grateful for the brief insight into Harrow Isle's history.

As I leave the shop, I make a note to myself to buy something from the shop when I have a chance. I continue wandering around town until I find myself standing in front of Harbor's Edge. I think about walking in there, but it is still pretty early. Coming back in the evening makes more sense and will give me an opportunity to meet more of the residents of Harrow Isle.

7

QUINN

As I sit in the driver's seat of the car I'm using while I'm here, a small draft of cold air from outside travels into the vehicle. I dig into my purse, pull out my wallet, and take out an old photograph. Its home has been in my wallet for years.

I stare at the photograph, haunted by the person captured in it. Their eyes are filled with love and their smile brings warmth to my heart.

The longer I stare at the photograph, the more I feel the queasiness growing in the pit of my stomach. Finding the picture of Laura and me in my room last night set off a chain of events that drew me to look at this photo again.

My heart races as I struggle to control the tears that threaten to fall from my eyes. Despite having years of experience with helping others navigate their inner demons, I still find myself getting caught up in the battles that I have against my own.

I shake my head in an attempt to rid myself of the negative thoughts that are coursing through my brain. With one last glance at the photograph, I fold it back up and put my wallet back in my purse. What that picture represents has nothing to do with what's going on right now and I need to focus on doing what I can to find Laura.

I step out of the car and zip up my coat because the cold air hits me ferociously. The town is eerily quiet, but based on my limited time here, I'm not surprised by it. The only thing I can hear in the distance is a soft murmur of waves crashing against the shore. As I walk toward The Harbor's Edge, I can't help but notice that the light emitting from it brings warmth to the darkness that surrounds this town. For some reason, I'm drawn to this place, but I can't explain why. After spending part of the day exploring what I could, it wouldn't hurt to see a spot where the locals hung out.

As I push open the door, the rich scent of woodsmoke and whiskey greets me. Warmth fills me as I take in this corner of the world. Intricate nautical maps and faded photographs line the walls, giving off an air of history and mystery, but that could just be my perception of it.

I make my way to the bar and take a seat on a worn leather stool. I glance at the variety of liquor bottles behind the bar, wondering if I should get a drink. A tall man with dark hair that is starting to have a sprinkle of gray is standing behind the counter. He immediately catches my attention as I study his broad shoulders, strong jawline, and rugged features that are softened by the warm lighting. When his blue eyes land on me, I can't help but feel intrigued by him. He walks over to me, and I adjust my position so I can look into his eyes easily.

"Evening," he starts. "First time here?"

"First time on the island or in Harbor's Edge?" I ask.

"Both."

"Yes, I assume it's probably pretty obvious."

He chuckles and I'm not sure if he's laughing at what I said or at me. Or it could be both. "I know most of the people who walk through those doors, and I definitely don't know you. Plus, there have been whispers about a newcomer among us." He pauses for a moment and then sticks his hand out. "Luke Hartley."

"Quinn Pierce," I reply, meeting his firm grip with one of my own. After what I'd heard this morning in the town square, I'm not surprised in the slightest that word about my arrival has made it to him.

"Welcome to Harbor's Edge."

It is then that I realize that this is the first time I have been welcomed to any part of this island. "Thank you."

"Can I get you a drink?"

"I'll take that beer." I use my hand to point to the one I'm talking about. "On tap, please."

He nods and I watch as the man in front of me pours the beer I requested into a glass. When he is done, he puts the glass down in front of me.

"What brings you here?" he asks as his eyes study me.

"Visiting, well, sort of. I'm a friend of Laura Bennett's," I say. I don't know how many people are aware of her disappearance. I need to be careful about how much information I give away. I take a sip of my beer, the refreshing taste calming me almost immediately.

"Ah, Laura," he murmurs, nodding slowly as if he is digesting what I said. "I heard about what happened."

"Do you know her?" I ask as I put my beer back down on the bar. I suspect that most people here know of each other, but whether they interact with each other is a different story.

"Eh, we exchange greetings, but it doesn't go too far beyond that," Luke admits. "I heard that she's gone missing."

I nod. "I'm here to find her."

"I wish I could help."

"But?" I ask, convinced that he is holding back.

He leans forward, bringing himself closer to me. I stop myself from moving back, determined to show that I am not afraid or intimidated by him entering my personal space. "Her husband would prefer that I stay away from her. Wouldn't be surprised if he got pissed I was talking to you either."

"That's strange," I say.

"Only if you're not from around here."

"Well then, Mr. Hartley. Why don't you enlighten me?"

A smirk plays on his lips before he speaks. "It would be my pleasure." He grabs a coaster and a glass that a patron left before turning back to me. "Harrow Isle is a place bound by tradition and history, including feuds that have lasted for generations."

"Continue."

He looks directly into my eyes, his gaze intense, but I meet it head-on. "My family and the Bennetts are two of the founding families of this island. And I swear we've been fighting ever since."

"Why?" I ask, wanting to understand the dynamics of the situation.

Luke hesitates and I can see that he is choosing his words carefully. "Power, influence, hell, arguing about whether the sky is blue or not. Our families have been at odds for decades."

I raise an eyebrow. "That's a long time."

He chuckles again, but this time, there's a hint of bitterness to it. "Oh, it is. Every time our families cross paths, I'm sure people are taking bets about whether a screaming match will break out. It was one of the reasons, but not the main reason, why I decided to join the military and get out of here. But I'm back now."

"Since Laura married Elliott, then she automatically became an enemy of your family and vice versa?"

Luke sighs, running a hand through his dark hair. "Correct."

I consider all of this for a moment. "So, are you considered a suspect in her disappearance?" It isn't the most tactful way to ask the question, but I need to know.

He does a double take before narrowing his gaze at me. "Of course not. Our families' rivalry has never stooped that low, and Sheriff Murray hasn't bothered to interview me about it."

"I'm just asking. Trying to find out as much as I can because all that matters to me is getting her home." I finish my statement by taking another sip of my beer.

"I can see that. How do you know Laura?"

"We went to college together. We were roommates freshman year and then stayed good friends until we graduated. Now I'm here to figure out what happened to her."

"That's understandable."

Silence falls between us as I consider what to say next. I appreciate him not getting offended by my accusation that he might be involved in whatever happened to Laura. Part of me begins hoping that someone else will need to order a drink or something and it will draw him away from me.

"Tell you what," Luke says, breaking the silence between us. "I'll give you a proper tour of the island tomorrow morning. There are some places you might find interesting, and maybe something might help with your investigation."

"Thank you, I appreciate that," I reply, relieved at not feeling completely alone, even though I'm still hesitant about whether I can trust him or not. "You're not worried about what Elliott will say about it if you're seen with me?"

"Not even a bit. Be ready by ten," he instructs, but his tone is gentle.

"I'll meet you here." I'm not too fond of being stuck with a stranger in their car.

"Sounds good."

I turn my head as the door to The Harbor's Edge creaks open, allowing a gust of cold air to invade the bar.

A man walks in, his tall frame filling the doorway. As he makes his way to the bar, his eyes, sharp and assessing, fall on me before sweeping across the room. As he approaches the bar and finds a seat, I can't help but notice the way his fingers tap an impatient rhythm on the countertop.

Luke takes a step away from me and turns to his new patron. "Evening, sheriff."

"Luke," the sheriff replies and then his gaze returns to me. "Ms. Pierce, I presume?"

"That's right," I confirm, swallowing hard as my heart races in my chest. There's something unnerving about the way he looks at me as if he's trying to determine my intentions. I'm not surprised that he knows who I am.

"I understand that Elliott Bennett called you here because of his wife's disappearance," Sheriff Murray says.

"That's also right. Is there a problem with that?" I ask cautiously, my instincts screaming at me to tread carefully.

"Only if you don't know what you're getting yourself into," he warns, his eyes never leaving mine. "Harrow Isle is a very small community, Ms. Pierce. We look out for one another, and we don't take kindly to outsiders stirring up trouble."

"Trouble?" I question, my grip tightening on my drink. "I just want to find out what happened to my friend."

"Then I suggest you approach this investigation with caution or just let me do my job," he advises. He turns to look at Luke. "I'd like my usual."

8

QUINN

As I stare up at the ceiling, my thoughts drift back to last night's conversation with Luke and Sheriff Murray, particularly his stern warning, which echoes in my mind.

Pushing aside the covers, I swing my legs over the edge of the bed and reach for Laura's phone on the nightstand. As I hold it in my hand, I remember the voice memos on it. I have more to listen to.

The next memo is a little longer than the previous one, so I take the phone to the bathroom and listen to it as I wash up. According to the date on the memo, this took place a couple of months after she moved to Harrow Isle.

The recording begins with the unmistakable noise of water in the background, the sound of waves gently breaking on the shore.

"Living on Harrow Isle is like a completely different world from New York City." A pause, then a chuckle follows. "In New York City, we were living the high life, going to events, living what many people would call a glamorous life. Here, things move much slower, and they enjoy solitude. Both places have their secrets though."

There's a soft sigh.

"Since I graduated from college, I haven't felt like I had a real friendship with anyone until I met Joanna. From the moment I stepped onto this island, she welcomed me with open arms when everyone else was relatively cold to me. Today was our first big argument, and I wasn't sure how to feel about it. Hopefully, once we have some time apart, things will go back to the way they were."

A rustle of fabric suggests she's shifting her body's positioning.

"And then there's Elliott. Moving here with him has been lovely for the most part. While I love and treasure him and our relationship, I want something more here."

Laura clears her throat, and I can't help but wonder if it's because she might be crying.

"All I want is to find genuine connections here with other people and to plant our roots here, but how will I if this town never warms up to me?"

The recording ends and I can't help but want more. I'm left wondering if things got better for her or not. I finish getting ready, and as I gather my belongings and make my way to the front door, I'm replaying the voice memo I just listened to over and over again in my head. Did Elliott know anything about how Laura had been feeling? Since Elliott listened to these before me, what did he think of them? How could he say that Laura is just rambling on them? Part of me wants to ask him, but then again, it isn't my business.

I walk downstairs and stare at the front door of the

Bennett mansion, knowing that once I step past the threshold, I'll feel a thousand times lighter.

My hand hesitates on the cold brass handle, but I push it down, ready to get out of this place.

"Quinn," a voice calls out from behind me, stopping me in my tracks. I turn to see Elliott standing just a few feet away. "Any updates about Laura? And where are you going?"

I'm taken aback by his questioning but understand his concern for his wife. "No, I don't have any updates, but I think I'm slowly starting to get an idea of certain aspects of her life here, especially through her voice memos. Right now, I'm on my way to Harbor's Edge because Luke Hartley is giving me a tour of Harrow Isle, and I'm hoping to get to know the town more," I reply, trying to sound casual but probably failing.

Elliott's eyes narrow, and he takes a step closer to me. "Be careful around him," he warns. "Luke has a reputation for being ruthless when it comes to getting what he wants."

I bite my tongue, holding back my response. I suspect Elliott's distrust of Luke stems from the long-standing feud between their families, but there's something in his tone that makes me wonder if there might be some truth to his words. Is there more here? Should I be more wary of Luke than I am? Or is this just another chapter in their family drama?

"Thank you for your concern," I say instead, not wanting to give away my own doubts. "But I can handle myself."

Elliott's gaze lingers on me for a moment longer than necessary. He then nods, seemingly accepting my decision. "Just remember what I said." And with that, he turns and walks away.

I also turn and leave the house, and I'm immediately greeted by sunlight. I get into the car and drive to Harbor's

Edge. Luckily, I'm able to get a parking spot right outside the bar, but I don't see Luke anywhere. I check the time and see that I'm a few minutes early, so I sit in the car and browse my phone until the clock strikes ten.

I'm so engrossed in my phone that I jump what feels like ten feet in the air when I hear a knock on my window. My head snaps toward the sound and I see Luke standing next to my car. I lower the window and I'm greeted by Luke and the cold.

"Ready for a tour?" Luke's voice is deep and soothing and I'm not sure how to feel about it.

"Ready as I'll ever be," I reply and add a somewhat forced smile. He gestures for me to get out of my car and soon I'm following him into town.

The sun does its part in helping us not be too cold as we walk through Harrow Isle. I can see where it could be charming, but the place still maintains a spooky vibe due to some of the weathered buildings. As we pass an old church with its crumbling stone walls, I can't help but think it is beautiful but haunting in a way. Luke points to a plaque by the entrance. I can barely read it because the plaque has faded due to time.

"Here is where one of the fights that began the Hartley-Bennett feud happened," he says.

"Wait. Are you kidding me? They fought at a church?"

"Yep. We're not even exactly sure what that fight was about."

"If you told me it was over a woman, I would completely believe you." I chuckle at the absurdity of it. "At least you somewhat know why you're feuding."

Luke grins and shakes his head. "That's one way to put it."

He sighs before he continues, "Our families were close friends once, believe it or not. What began here turned into something that neither side has been able to get over. Shall we continue?"

I nod, and together we walk down the street side by side. By mistake, my hand brushes against his and I jump slightly but try to do it discreetly, so Luke doesn't know. But when his eyes reach mine, I know I've been caught, but thankfully he doesn't mention it.

"Over there is our public library. It's one of the oldest buildings on the island."

It isn't hard to believe that. Though its condition is much better than the old church we passed.

Luke continues speaking when I don't utter a sound. "There are books, of course, but the collection includes a multitude of things, old manuscripts, journals, newspaper clippings. It's a beacon of history."

"I'll have to check it out while I'm here," I say as I turn my head to look up at him.

"You might be surprised at what you'll find."

We leave the library and continue walking. We pass by cute shops and a café where I can smell freshly baked pastries. It is completely different from what I'd seen when I arrived on Harrow Isle. I'd seen a glimpse of this when I was near the antique shop, but having a tour guide makes me appreciate the scenery more.

"I couldn't imagine being angry at someone to the point where it was passed down for generations," I say, watching an old man feed birds in Harrow Isle's town square.

Then again, that might be a lie. I will always hate the person who was responsible for changing my life forever.

However, I'm not sure if I'm going to be passing down any hatred for that person since I don't have any children.

Luke shrugs. "Some things are harder to get over. The island might look peaceful right now, but there is an ugly side, Quinn. There are invisible lines people don't cross."

I think about Laura and her mysterious disappearance. "Did Laura cross one of those lines?"

He glances at me, his blue eyes searching mine, before looking away. "I can't answer that. But from what I hear from others, Laura saw Harrow Isle through rose-colored glasses, and that was both a blessing and a curse."

Silence settles between us as I replay what he just said over and over again. As Luke and I continue on our tour, I can't help but feel that Laura's disappearance is somehow intertwined with Harrow Isle's history, but how and by whom?

Could it be Luke? He hasn't made any threatening moves toward me to indicate that is what he has in mind, but that could be him attempting to lure me into his trap.

"Over there is the old mill," his voice cuts through my thoughts as he gestures to a crumbling building. "A fire broke out there one night a long time ago, killing everyone inside. While I don't have any experience with this, some say you can still hear their screams."

"That is absolutely horrible. There is a lot of pain in general here."

When Luke doesn't respond, I get the feeling that he agrees with me.

Just as we are about to walk around a corner, we come face-to-face with a woman who looks to be slightly older than me, with long brown hair and hazel eyes. I recognize her immediately from the photos Laura posted on social media.

"Luke, it's lovely to see you." There is a hint of surprise in her voice.

"Joanna," Luke says in return. He glances at me out of the corner of his eye before looking back at her. "This is Quinn, Laura's college roommate. She's here to help find her. Quinn, this is Joanna, Laura's best friend."

I keep my cool as I remember Laura's voice memo about her argument with Joanna, but the voice memo is months old. It isn't out of the realm of possibility that they patched things up by now.

A flash of genuine concern crosses Joanna's face. "We're all worried about her." She hesitates for a moment, looking out at Harrow Isle's town square before turning back to us. I can see that she is trying to find the right words to say. "I just hope she's alright... wherever she is."

I blow out a deep breath. "I can't imagine how hard this must be for you."

Joanna's gaze meets mine. "Laura is... complicated, but I didn't expect this to happen. She had been acting strange for the last several weeks leading up to her disappearance."

That sparks my interest because it is news to me. "Strange how?"

"She became more withdrawn. In most instances, she was the life of the party, but all of that seemed to dull considerably in the time leading up to when she disappeared."

That is interesting. When Elliott and I spoke, he didn't mention anything about her behavior being unusual leading up to her disappearance. In fact, he made it seem as if everything was normal.

"Did she mention anything about going somewhere? Someplace she might have wanted to see and visit?"

Joanna shakes her head, and I can see the shift in her eyes just before she says, "Look, maybe it's best that you let the police handle it. There's a lot about Harrow Isle and its people that outsiders don't understand. Be careful, Quinn. Not just for your sake, but for Laura's."

I'm taken aback by Joanna's warning. "I appreciate the advice."

Joanna's eyes reach Luke's. "Just be careful."

Her gaze lands on me briefly, and I can't read the expression on her face. Without another word, Joanna walks away, leaving Luke and me alone once again.

A few moments pass, and Luke and I don't say a word. The only thing standing between us is Joanna's warning because it's still hanging in the air.

Finally, I turn to look at Luke and ask, "Do you have any idea what that was all about?"

Luke folds his arms across his chest and says, "Not a clue."

9

LAURA

Six Months Ago

With a heavy heart, I let out a shaky breath. The isolation of Harrow Isle feels unbearable at times like these, a stark contrast to the vibrant energy of my former life in New York City. There, I was surrounded by people I wasn't sure I could trust, caught up in the whirlwind of social events and philanthropic ventures that defined my place in the city that never sleeps. Here, however, I still feel as if I'm nothing but a stranger in a place I've now lived in for months. Although you wouldn't really be able to tell if I'd lived here because the only place I'd added my touch to is my office.

Tonight, we are sitting at our dining room table, enjoying our dinner by candlelight. It would be romantic if not for the awkwardness between us. Elliott, pausing between bites, posed a familiar question, "Are you happy here?"

Without missing a beat, I say, "Of course." It has become an instinctual response to his question that I know he'll ask at least once a month, sometimes once a week. What makes this evening different is Elliott's response to mine.

"Perhaps it would help if you got to know the island better," he says, tossing it out as if it were that simple. "You've spent a lot of time by yourself, outside of hanging out with Joanna."

"You're right," I reply, surprising even myself. There is a sudden determination that I haven't felt since we arrived here. "I think I'll do some exploring tomorrow. Will you join me?"

"I won't be able to, sweetheart. Work obligations. But maybe we can do something this weekend?"

I smile at him, happy because of the prospect of spending time with him. "That sounds like a plan."

"Be careful," Elliott warns, and it forces me to look at him. There's something in his eyes that I can't quite explain, but it leaves me feeling uneasy.

"I will," I promise, and I intend to keep my word.

The next evening, I'm in my office recovering from dinner and a long day exploring Harrow Isle. I notice a few drops of rain on my window as I pick up my phone and start to speak.

"I—I still feel trapped here on Harrow Isle. Elliott's promise of a fresh start here and an effort to escape the ruthless pace of New York City has fallen flat. Although our lives have slowed down, I feel as if I've traded one prison for another."

Tears are hanging on to the corners of my eyes by a thread as I think about my situation. It feels foolish to be crying about this, given how much I have and how fortunate I am.

But here I am, talking to myself, barely holding on to the dam that is threatening to break.

I want to talk to someone. I need to talk to someone who will understand.

My thoughts drift to Joanna, the closest thing I have to a friend on this island. "I wish I could confide in Joanna." I pause for a second to collect myself. "But there's something about her that makes me hesitate, and I don't know what it is.

"The one bright spot is that I spent the day exploring Harrow Isle. It was enlightening, to say the least, and I'm nowhere near done. There's something about this place that I can't firmly grasp. I found out about some of the history of the island, some things that Elliott failed to mention to me in all the time we've been dating and married.

"I'm starting to piece together some of this place's history, which I'm convinced is haunting everyone who lives here on the island. And I believe my husband's family is tied up in it. Elliott hasn't said the words, but the time I've spent exploring and then at the library is telling me so. But why wouldn't he tell me? That's the question that currently plagues my mind, but I'm not prepared to ask Elliott yet. However, that's not all."

I pause for a second to catch my breath and just as I'm about to speak, there's a soft knock on the door, interrupting me. My head snaps up and I look in the direction of the sound.

"Come in," I announce, but no one does. I swallow hard as a small surge of panic flies through me.

I continue to stare at the door and then say, "Elliott?" My hopes are dashed when he doesn't enter the room.

Slowly, I rise from my chair and walk toward the door. "Is

someone there? You can come in," I say, but no one enters. But that's not the end of this because I can hear the sound of the floor creaking under someone or something.

My hand hovers just above the doorknob, wondering if I am ready to confront whoever is on the other side of the door. Everything within me is screaming not to. I drop my hand and it lands on the doorknob. Without taking another second to think about it, I grip the doorknob hard and swing the door open.

10

Present Day

I am willing to bet the walls of this room are closing in on me. It's a sensation I recognize from many of my clients, often indicating anxiety or a response to trauma. I also have personal experience with this, but the timing of it surprises me. I take a deep breath, trying to ground myself in the moment. It's important that I draw on the mindfulness techniques I often teach in my sessions.

My fingers tremble slightly as they hover over the phone. I summon the courage, and finally, I press play again on Laura's voice memo. Her voice fills the room and I'm transported back into the memory she recorded.

"I—I still feel trapped here on Harrow Isle. Elliott's promise of a fresh start here and an effort to escape the ruthless pace of New York City has fallen flat. Although our lives have slowed down, I feel as if I've traded one prison for another."

I place the phone back down on the bedside table. I close my eyes as I try to envision Laura speaking into the phone. The worry in her voice is apparent, and it only makes me grow more concerned, and to make matters worse, this voice memo was from six months ago. Have things grown worse since?

When the recording ends once more, a shiver crawls down my spine. Who had shown up at her door? There is a chance I would never know, but I need to focus on what I can control.

I can't help but think back to the library. Luke had mentioned its vast collection of books and historical records and Laura mentioned visiting there. I wonder if there might be clues or something hidden there. Clues that could lead me to Laura or at least tell me if she discovered anything after she began her journey to learn about the history of Harrow Isle.

Going to the library isn't guaranteed to lead me to anything, but right now, it's the only thing that I have to go on. If the Bennetts and Hartleys are the founders of the island, it must contain information on them.

The voice memo has done more than lure me to the library. I swear that I can hear my internal clock ticking as more time passes since Laura left. It has also sent my mind into a tailspin as I wonder who I should trust. It is clear to me that, at least at one point, Elliott was keeping secrets from Laura. But why would he do so? He is also the last one who saw her before she was gone, and I only have his version of events leading up to her disappearance.

That leads to another question popping into my head. How much should I share with him about what I'm finding out?

"Can I trust him?" I say out loud to myself, rubbing my arms as a chill covers my body. My relationship with Elliott so far has been cordial but distant. I don't expect us to be friends, but it feels as if he's barely interacted with me since I arrived.

"Maybe he's just as concerned as I am, and it's causing him to act frosty toward me," I say as I try to reason with myself. "But could it be that he is involved?"

My thoughts begin to spiral. At best, he could have kidnapped her. At worst, he has committed murder, but what would be the point in bringing me here if that were the case?

I shake my head because I don't want to entertain these dark assumptions without having evidence. Yet I can't deny that something about him feels off.

I need to find out more information before talking to Elliott.

I check the time before walking over to my bed and slipping under the covers. I might have a long day tomorrow and need all the rest I can get. I turn off the lamp and do my best to get to sleep.

However, sleep refuses to come easily. My thoughts continue to swirl around Laura's voice and the contents of the voice memo. I can't help but lie there, eyes wide open, staring into the darkness that now surrounds me.

Nothing I do helps my attempts to calm myself enough to fall asleep.

"Something else is wrong here," I admit out loud. "And I don't know what it is."

I turn over for what has to be the thousandth time. I'm afraid to look at the time because I know it's been hours since I went to bed. It is then that I remember an old therapy technique I'd often share with anxious clients, grounding exercises. I focus on five things I can see, four I can touch, three I can hear, two I can smell, and one I can taste. The rhythm of the exercise starts to calm me down, but the grip that all of this has on me remains.

However, the weight of my tiredness presses down on me until, finally, exhaustion takes over and I fall asleep.

11

QUINN

I shut the car door as the bright sun beams down on my face. The warmth from the sun is somewhat soothing to me, but the weight of my expectations for today still weighs heavily on me.

As I walk toward the library, I clutch the strap of my bag tighter because it's holding a bunch of the things I'll need if today goes as expected, including my laptop, pens, papers, and both phones.

I quickly walk up the stone steps and push open one of the heavy wooden doors. I cringe as the creak of the door echoes throughout the quiet space.

I give a small smile to the librarian standing at the front desk and she hesitantly returns it, reminding me that, once again, I'm an outsider here. I look around and my eyes land on someone familiar. Before I can stop myself, I walk over to the person.

"Hey, Luke," I say, trying my best to keep my voice low, keeping in mind where we are.

Luke is sitting at a reading table near the entrance of the

library. A book rests in his hands, but once he looks up, his expression brightens.

"Hey," he says as I adjust the strap of my purse on my shoulder. "What are you doing here?"

"After our tour yesterday, I figured it would be a great opportunity to learn more about the history of Harrow Isle," I say without hesitation. It's not a complete lie, but I'm not telling the whole truth either.

"I'm glad the tour served as some inspiration," he says.

Part of me knows I can't afford to get distracted by him, but the other half of me thinks it would be rude to leave without at least spending a couple of seconds to say hello. It doesn't take much to guess which side won.

"Are you okay?"

I'm startled by his question. I look around before my eyes land back on him. "Yeah. I think so. Why?"

"Just asking."

Could he really read me that easily? I don't know how I feel about that and the thought of him being able to do that doesn't sit well with me. That makes me want to run away from him as fast as I can.

"Hey, I don't want to take up too much of your time, but I assume I'll see you around?"

Luke nods and gives me a small grin. "You definitely will."

It isn't until I'm halfway across the floor that I realize that I have no idea where I'm going.

I look around and take note of the library's layout, including the various sections dedicated to different subjects. I want to explore a little first before diving into what I assume will be an online catalog that will point me to the exact place that I need to be. Immediately, my eyes are drawn to the local history section. I start looking through the books in the section when someone near me speaks.

"Can I help you? Are you looking for something?" a soft voice breaks my concentration.

I turn to find a woman standing next to me. Her silver hair is pulled back into a low bun and she's wearing business casual clothes. Already she seems to be nicer than the shopkeeper I met at the antique shop.

When I've stared at her for a bit too long, I shake my head. "Sorry, I'm new here. I'm hoping to find out more about Harrow Isle's history."

"Welcome, I'm Mrs. Smith and I'm one of the librarians here."

I hold out my hand for her to shake. "I'm Quinn." I decide not to fill her in on why I'm here. Thankfully, she doesn't ask any more questions.

"There's no shortage of stories about this island. Some believe it's a beautiful destination; others believe it is cursed. The truth lies somewhere in between, I suppose," she says as she guides me to a particular section. She gestures to a couple of shelves. "Right here is where some of our history books are."

I take a step closer to the books to read the titles as Mrs. Smith pulls out a worn, leather-bound book. "This one contains accounts of strange occurrences and local legends from the last two centuries if that is of interest to you."

"Thank you," I say, accepting the book. As I flip through the yellowed pages, I know I need to take a closer look at this one.

"Now, if you'll excuse me, I have to get back to the front desk, but please let me know if I can help with anything else."

With that, she turns and walks away, leaving me alone with the knowledge that my time researching here has only just begun.

It takes some time, but I read and skim through several books before slamming one closed a little harder than necessary. Some of the history I learned about Harrow Isle is interesting, but there is nothing groundbreaking about the island or its founders. Most of what I could find was about how much the Bennetts have harmed the residents of Harrow Isle over the years and now the descendants were cursed.

I get up and walk over to a computer to look through some old news articles to see if they might be able to tell me things that some of the books might have skipped or skimmed over.

I'm pretty impressed that older editions of the town's newspaper have been uploaded to the library's database, potentially making it easier for me to search through them.

Beginning my search, I type in a few keywords related to people suddenly vanishing and choose to skim the headlines from various decades. I make a note to myself to look up anything related to the Bennetts and Hartleys if I come up empty-handed after this. A headline from the 1990s catches my eye: "Local Woman Vanishes Without a Trace." The article recounts what they think were the last days of Stephanie Marsh, who was last seen near The Harbor's Edge. The police searched for her, but they didn't find any leads and her case went cold.

I take the opportunity to write down facts about the case before I continue searching.

Another article from the 2000s piques my interest. It talks about a writer who had come here to learn more about

Harrow Isle and get inspiration for an upcoming novel but then suddenly disappeared from the island. I write down details about the case and how the person, dead or alive, had never been found.

I pull up more articles, and soon the pattern becomes clear. Every decade or so, someone disappears on Harrow Isle. The circumstances differ, but the point still remains the same—for such a small community, having disappearances like this is odd. This is circumstantial evidence at best, but I can't stop the thoughts that are now swirling through my head.

Pushing back from the desk, the gravity of the situation hits me. Laura's disappearance is more than likely not just some random event. It's tied to a series of people vanishing over the years. A shiver creeps down my spine, forcing me to shake involuntarily. I could be right in the middle of serial kidnappings or murders, and if that's the case, what are the chances that Laura is alive?

As I push back from the desk, I take a deep breath, trying to process what I've just found. Beyond the headlines and statistics, these are human lives, stories left unfinished. Laura's disappearance isn't a singular incident. It seems as if it's a tradition of sorts here. I've studied cases and patterns and human behavior, but now, more than ever, I feel as if I'm in way over my head.

I can't even begin to wrap my head around researching anything else. Maybe I'm jumping to conclusions, but I need to get out of here and fast.

I grab my things and haphazardly throw them into my bag. I speed walk through the library and just as I'm about to leave, I hear someone say, "Miss?"

I turn and find Mrs. Smith standing behind me.

"If you want to speak to someone about the history of Harrow Isle"—she pauses, as if debating whether to share this information —"Abigail Cook. She lives on the outskirts of town and has been here longer than most of us. I'm confident that she knows things no one else knows."

"Abigail Cook?" I repeat, curiosity piqued. A name I haven't heard before. "How do I find her?"

"Take the path behind the church and follow it until you reach a cottage near the cliffs. But be warned, she doesn't take kindly to strangers."

That is why she was concerned about telling me about her. "Thank you, Mrs. Smith," I say as I take out my phone to quickly jot down the directions.

I slip the phone back into my purse, my fingers trembling as I think about what I just found on the library's computer. I leave the library, this time not even caring about the creaky door. I welcome the sun and the cool air that drifts across my face because I feel as if my face is flushed after what I just discovered.

"Hey, Quinn." Luke's voice startles me. I turn to see him standing behind me, his expression showing nothing but concern. "You all right?"

"Y—yeah," I say, forcing a smile. "This is the second time you've asked me that today."

Luke studies me for a moment, his blue eyes seeming to pierce through me. He takes a step toward me and says, "I can tell something's bothering you, especially right now."

"Thanks, Luke," I whisper, touched by his kindness.

"Would a change of scenery help take your mind off... this momentarily?"

"Wait. What do you mean?"

"How about we grab dinner? Maybe tonight if you're available?"

I blink at him twice before I respond. "Yes, I'd love that."

Guilt immediately fills me because it would mean taking time out of my search for Laura, but maybe it would give me an opportunity to relax somewhat.

"Let's exchange numbers, and I'll give you the details in about an hour or so?"

"Sounds perfect," I say, and I truly mean it. I give him a smile and then notice something out of the corner of my eye. I turn my head slightly, and for a split second, I think I see something in one of the upper windows of the library. But when I do a double take and look again, it's gone.

12

QUINN

As I stand in front of the mirror, smoothing down a simple black dress that I'd haphazardly thrown into my suitcase just before zipping it up, my thoughts drift back to Laura. A pang of guilt gnaws at me; should I even be thinking about a date, let alone going out on one when Laura is still missing?

I shake off the feeling, reminding myself that I need allies here. Luke could be a valuable one. He knows the ins and outs of Harrow Isle. Maybe something he knows will help me find Laura.

I apply my lipstick to my lips before grabbing my purse and my coat and heading to the front door of the Bennett mansion. As I'm putting my coat on, I see Mrs. Fleming standing in the living room, staring at me, but when my eyes meet hers, she turns on her heel and walks away.

When I step out into the cool night air, I shake off the feeling that I'm being watched in the Bennett household and continue on my way to the car that I'm borrowing from Elliott.

Speaking of, at least he isn't here to question me about where I am going and if it includes Luke. Given that this is a small town, I suspect that news about Luke and me will reach Elliott before I get back here. The drive to the restaurant is uneventful, and soon I'm getting out of my car and standing just a block away from where I'm supposed to be.

The restaurant is tucked between a couple of quaint shops, which have already closed for the night. Thankfully, the outside of this place is more lit than the area around The Harbor's Edge, so I don't feel uneasy about walking there.

As I step inside the establishment, my senses are greeted with the smell of garlic and other spices and herbs. The dim lighting creates an intimate atmosphere, and I can immediately feel the vibe that Luke is going for.

I walk up to the hostess desk and tell them who I'm meeting for dinner. It takes a few seconds, but suddenly my eyes meet Luke's as I'm walking toward our table. I'm doing my best to appear calm and collected, despite the internal conflict about a multitude of things raging within me.

"Good evening, Luke," I say as he stands up to greet me.

He gives me a small hug before pulling out the chair next to his instead of the one that is across. It takes me less than ten seconds to become aware of how close we're sitting. His rough hand grazes mine as he thanks the hostess and passes me the menu.

"You look beautiful tonight, Quinn."

I look up from the menu, only just starting to read and smile at him. "Thank you."

We sit there in silence for a couple of minutes, trying to decide what we're going to eat before we take a deep dive into a conversation that will do nothing but distract us from the rest of the world. Once we are done and order our meals and drinks, I turn to Luke and say, "Have you lived on Harrow Isle your entire life?"

"Sort of. Was born and raised here, then left because I joined the military. Then I moved back here," he says, taking a sip of his water. "My family's been on this island for generations though, as you know."

He was alluding to the feud, something I really didn't want to talk about at this second. "What made you want to come back and open a bar?"

"I took it over from my father and… I guess I was looking for a fresh start," he admits with a sigh. "Besides, my family is still here, and I wanted to be close to my roots and help them if need be."

"Speaking of roots and history," I venture, hoping to shift things to one of the reasons I wanted to go out with him in the first place, "I've heard and read some strange things about Harrow Isle."

"Ah, yes." Luke chuckles darkly, leaning back in his chair. "We certainly have our fair share of weird stories and tales."

Luke stops talking when our waiter gives us two glasses of red wine. We both quickly say thank you and Luke picks up his glass. "There have been unexplained events on this island. Things disappearing and disappearances, strange lights in the fog."

"Disappearances?" I ask. "Like people?"

"There have been a few over the years, some before my time," he admits, shifting uncomfortably in his seat. "But most of us suspect the people just left the island without the town knowing. Then again, who knows, you know?"

I know. Because all the stories I found of people disappearing ended up as cold cases.

I'm not sure how much of what Luke is saying is just part of the hearsay that is passed down among the residents of this island, but it's hard to shake the feeling that there might be more darkness to these stories than he is letting on or knows.

"Enough about Harrow Isle," Luke says, breaking through my thoughts. "Let's talk about something else. What do you do for a living?"

"I'm a therapist."

"What made you want to become a therapist?"

"Um, well," I begin, taken aback by the sudden shift in conversation. "I guess I've always felt a connection to people, a desire to help them navigate their struggles. And after experiencing my own trauma, it further drove my need to help others."

"This might be too dark for a first date, but what happened, if you don't mind sharing?" He raises an eyebrow and although I don't want to talk about this, I appreciate how gentle he's being about the whole thing.

"It's not something I like to talk about," I say, trying to keep my tone light as a way to deflect from my past. "What about you? Was the military always part of your plan?"

"Plan?" He chuckles, shaking his head. "Never really had one of those when I was younger. I joined up because it seemed like the best way to escape this place for a while. See the world, you know?"

"Did it live up to your expectations?"

"Sometimes," he admits as he adjusts himself in his chair.

"But there's no place like home, even when home is Harrow Isle."

Our conversation drifts from topic to topic even when our dinner is delivered. I can feel a bond growing between us as we talk about our personal histories and the history of Harrow Isle. Time flies by and I find myself grateful for Luke's company.

"Thanks for tonight, Luke," I say as we finish our meal. "It's been a wonderful evening."

"You're more than welcome," he says as he signs the check that had only come to our table moments before. Once everything is squared away, we stand up, put our coats on, and make our way toward the exit.

"Would you like to go on a walk?" Luke asks as we step out of the restaurant, the night air cool against my face.

"Sure," I agree, eager to prolong this evening as much as I can. As we stroll down the streets of Harrow Isle, I can't help but notice how the moon casts an eerie glow over this town.

At first, the only sound between us is our footsteps, which are punctuated by the crash of waves against the cliffs. Despite walking around Harrow Isle, which has an unsettling atmosphere in the daylight as well as at nighttime, there's something undeniably romantic about the way this night is wrapping up, including this walk.

Luke and I are quietly talking among ourselves. When I try to respond to his comment, I stop in my tracks when I find someone coming out of the shadows and notice she's coming toward us.

Her body is wrapped in layers of shawls. I take a step closer to Luke because I'm not sure what's going to happen. Her piercing gaze locks onto mine as she hobbles toward us, her movements slow but deliberate. My pulse quickens, the air around us seems to thicken with tension.

"Be careful," the elderly woman says as she looks directly at me. "You've come seeking answers, but some doors are best left shut. Tightly."

"I'm just looking for answers about what happened to Laura."

Her gaze lingers on me a moment longer. "Not everything is as it seems, and not everyone is who they claim to be."

With that, she walks around us and off into the night.

"That was Abigail Cook," Luke says, breaking the silence between us. "She's lived on Harrow Isle longer than anyone else."

I'm surprised to find out her identity, but her warning sends the romantic evening we are having out in a downward spiral. But I do know I will need to talk to Abigail sooner rather than later now.

13

QUINN

As I pull up to Abigail Cook's cottage, the gloomy sky casts a dark shadow over the worn-down exterior. Despite the state of the exterior of the house, there is still a certain charm that I can't quite describe.

I open the car door and glance around. The wind blowing through the trees and the distant crash of waves against the shore do nothing but heighten the sense of isolation. As I walk up to the porch, the front door swings open, taking me by surprise. The elderly woman who I briefly saw last night stares straight into my soul, making me wonder if coming here is a good idea or not.

"Ms. Pierce," Abigail greets me as I walk up the final step. "I've been expecting you."

"Ms. Cook," I reply, masking my unease about this encounter and her knowing my name with a polite smile. Flashes of my brief run-in with her last night while out on my date with Luke appear in my mind. That was creepy as well.

"Please call me Abigail. Come inside," she says, gesturing for me to enter her home.

As I step over the threshold, I can't help but notice the odd assortment of trinkets that fill her small living room. There's a small amount of furniture, but books upon books line several bookshelves in this room while faded photographs hang on the walls. If I thought I'd stepped back in time when I arrived at Harrow Isle, it's nothing compared to this.

"Can I get you something to drink? Water? Tea?" Abigail asks, interrupting my thoughts.

"It's totally okay. I don't need anything."

Abigail gives me a small smile. "I'm already going to get something for myself. It's not a problem."

"Water would be lovely, thank you," I reply, taking a seat in one of her armchairs. My mind races with questions as I watch Abigail walk out of the room. How had she known to expect me? What does she know about the history of this island? How about the feud between the Bennetts and the Hartleys?

Abigail comes back with a glass of water for me, and I assume a cup of tea for herself. Once she hands it to me, she sits down in the chair across from mine.

"Strange things happen on this island," Abigail says as she settles into a chair opposite me. "But then again, you already knew that, didn't you, Ms. Pierce?"

"Feel free to call me Quinn."

"Quinn, that's a very pretty name, but I'm sure you didn't come here for pleasantries."

She is right. I didn't.

She doesn't give me a chance to respond because she speaks once again. "I'm sure you've heard the old saying, 'The truth is hidden in plain sight.' Well, that applies to a lot of the history about Harrow Isle."

Intrigued, I lean forward, my fingers gripping the delicate glass. "What do you mean?"

She smiles at me and I'm not sure how to feel about it. "You see, the founding families have deep roots that run throughout the island's history. They helped build the foundation which we continue to prosper from. However, sometimes the roots can strangle as much as they anchor."

What is she hinting at? But before I can ask a question, she gives me another smile.

"Would you like some more water?" Abigail asks. Her tone is now warm and casual. It's a stark contrast to the darkness that surrounded her riddle. I glance down and notice I haven't taken a sip.

"Abigail," I say cautiously, "I appreciate learning whatever you wish to tell me, but I need more clarity. What exactly are you trying to tell me about the Bennetts and the Hartleys?"

"Ah, so you have done your homework." She folds her hands in her lap. "If you're interested in finding out more about our history and 'the feud,' I'm happy to share some of the things I know. The Bennetts have always been ambitious, eager to maintain their position at the top of Harrow Isle society. Throughout the years, they've used their wealth and influence to secure their place, often resorting to"—she pauses and looks up at the ceiling as if she is searching for the right word—"unsavory methods."

"Unsavory?" I ask. "What kind of methods are we talking about?"

"Take the lighthouse, for example," she says, her voice dropping to almost a whisper. "It was once owned by a family who didn't like the Bennetts. But after a series of unfortunate incidents, robbery, fire, etc., they were left with no choice but to sell. And who should buy it? The Bennetts."

"No way that was a coincidence, right?"

"If you want to call it a coincidence, they seem to have a habit of occurring when it benefits the Bennetts most. The lighthouse is just one example."

"Has anyone called out the Bennetts for what they are doing? Has anyone been able to stand up against them for these... incidents?"

"The issue is that nothing can be proven," she replies, her eyes gleaming with an eerie intensity. "People have tried, and then another incident happens. The only people who have been able to stand up to them and survive are the Hartleys, but I wouldn't be surprised if there was something more brewing now. Tensions are high. Hold on, I want to show you something."

I watch as she walks away, and I'm left reeling from her revelations as the pieces start to fall into place. If what Abigail is talking about even remotely contains a shred of truth, there's more at play here than I ever imagined.

Moments later, she returns with a worn photo album tucked under her arm.

"Here," she says, carefully turning the pages until she finds what she's looking for. "Take a look at this."

My gaze falls upon an old black-and-white photograph depicting what I assume is a younger Abigail standing beside a man who bears a striking resemblance to Elliott Bennett. They looked... happy.

"That looks like Elliott."

"It's Theodore Bennett, his grandfather," she replies, a sad smile tugging at the corners of her mouth. "We were quite close once upon a time. Though our paths diverged many years ago. I've kept this photo for so long because it's hard to forget someone who was so much a part of your life, no matter how much time has passed."

Her words resonate with me as I think about the photo I carry around in my purse. Each time I glance at it, her face staring back at me evokes a blend of emotions, but the pain always seems to win. For now, I need to push my past grief to the side and focus on what is at stake here.

"Abigail," I say, struggling to keep my voice steady. "What can you tell me about this photograph? When was it taken?"

"Ah, that would be just after my twenty-first birthday," she reminisces, her gaze turning distant. "Theodore was already making a name for himself in the family business here and abroad. We were both young and carefree, believing we could change the world—or at least our little corner of it."

"Did you ever suspect him of being involved in what you've told me?" The question hangs heavy in the air, and I can sense Abigail carefully weighing her response.

"Yes, because it was what he'd been taught that he needed to do in life. He had to do whatever it took to eliminate any obstacles in his way. At all costs."

It takes everything in me to stop my jaw from dropping open. "Are you insinuating that the Bennetts—"

Abigail cuts me off with a shake of her head. "All I'm saying is, with power and privilege, there can be a big cost. And the Bennetts have always been willing to pay that price, no matter the cost or who they have to take down in order to do it."

I take a deep breath to steady my nerves before I say what

is on the tip of my tongue. The articles that I found at the library swirl in the corner of my mind. "Would they go as far as to kidnap or murder?"

Abigail's eyes dart away momentarily before reaching mine once again. "I've lived long enough to know that when someone's backed into a corner, especially with their reputation on the line, they're capable of anything."

The bomb that Abigail just dropped on me is enough to incinerate my entire world. Not only could Laura already be dead, but there is a chance I'm currently staying with her murderer. But what doesn't make sense is why he would invite me here if he has something to do with Laura's disappearance.

I am still trying to make sense of all of this, so I decide to try a different line of questioning. "Do you know why I'm interested in the history of Harrow Isle?"

The question is somewhat vague, but that is on purpose. Abigail knows way more than she's telling me and I'm willing to bet she knows why I'm here.

"I know that this is personal for you. You're here for a stronger reason than just visiting on vacation."

She leans in closer to me, creating an atmosphere of confidentiality between us. "It's not common for someone to take such an interest unless there's a deeper connection. Especially when it comes to the Bennetts and the Hartleys because that is what I believe you really came here to learn more about."

I hesitate as I rub a hand along my lip, debating whether to reveal my cards. Finally, I decide on a mix of truth and vagueness. "Elliott's wife, Laura. She's my friend from college and I'm trying to help him find her."

The old woman's face changes ever so slightly. Most people probably wouldn't have noticed the change, but I do. "Ah, Laura," she murmurs thoughtfully. "A lovely young woman who mostly kept to herself. She and Elliott seemed so perfect together. Deep down, I hoped it would break the Bennetts' curse that seems to control them, forcing them to want to maintain power at all costs. But love, like all things on this island, can be deceptive."

She lets the words hang in the air for a moment, allowing me to absorb them. "You were close to her?" she asks, though it feels more like a statement than a question.

"We were while in college, but I could have done a better job of maintaining contact with her in the years since. We haven't spoken in a couple of years. Elliott asked me to come down and help find her if she's still on the island."

Abigail's gaze never wavers from mine. "I think what you might end up finding is that Laura's story is interwoven with the history of this island. Be cautious in your quest to find her and for answers, Quinn. Some truths might be better left buried."

I lick my now dry lips as I feel the weight of her words. There's so much she isn't saying, but I think I'm starting to connect the dots, and all of this might be way more than I can handle.

"Dear, I have an appointment that I need to get to soon, and it takes me much longer to get to places than it used to in my youth."

I nod as I stand up. "I can bring these dishes back to the kitchen for you to save you an extra step."

Abigail waves me off. "Don't worry about it. I'll get to it later."

"Thank you for sharing all of this with me," I say, struggling to wrap my head around this new information. I grab my purse and start walking to the door, with Abigail trailing slightly behind me.

"Take care now and be very careful," she says as she opens the door for me. "You never know who is watching."

I nod and step outside. As I'm walking to my car, the wind whips around me, chilling me to the bone. I wrap my coat tighter around myself and continue toward my car. My mind races due to what I've just learned and my interactions with Elliott.

His behavior over the phone and then in person sit on completely opposite sides of the spectrum, and I haven't been able to understand it until now. My fingers tighten around the car remote as I think about what all of this means. There's no denying it, and I wish it weren't so, but Elliott has become a person of interest in Laura's disappearance.

As I slide into the driver's seat and start the engine, my phone rings. I yank my purse open and pick up the phone. I glance down at the screen and sigh, thankful it's not Elliott.

"Hello?"

"Hey, it's Luke. Just wanted to see how you're doing today."

"Luke," I exhale, grateful for the sound of his voice. "I'm fine. Thanks for checking in."

"No problem. I was thinking about our date last night and wanted to know if you wanted to go out again sometime soon?"

I think about it for a second before I give my answer. "Yes, I would love that. Can we decide on a day later on? I'm about to drive back to the Bennett mansion."

"Sounds good. I'll reach out to you later."

I smile briefly. "Thanks. I'll talk to you then."

I hang up the phone, and as I put it back into my purse, my fingers brush against a folded piece of paper. Puzzled, I pull it out and unfold it. The texture is thin and smooth, like your typical printer paper, but I don't remember putting it in there. However, with everything that has been happening lately, it's possible I simply forgot.

The message on the paper is handwritten in an elegant, cursive script in black ink. I read the note out loud. "The deeper you dig, the darker it gets. Tread lightly."

I read it to myself once more, stunned at what I am holding. Who could have left this note? And when did they do it?

I glance around, searching for any sign of someone watching me or lurking nearby, but I see no one.

Had Abigail snuck it into my purse? But she hadn't been alone with my things while I was in her home.

If it wasn't her, then who was it?

14

QUINN

A dull glow covers the room I'm in and I can barely make out who and what is in here around me. I look to my left and find Laura sitting at a vintage writing desk with her red scarf around her neck. I can't see her face, but the scarf is a giveaway. Her hands move furiously, scribbling on what looks like a notepad.

I take a step as the wooden floorboards creak below me, wishing that I could see what she was writing. When I try to take another step, I freeze as a young girl's laughter floats through the room. It's familiar, yet distant.

I turn to see a small figure, her back to me, playing with a baby doll that looks almost identical to one I had as a child. The child's hair looks so much like mine had when I was that age. I wonder if I should walk over to the little girl, but I turn and see Laura still writing at the desk.

"Laura!" I try to shout, but I can't. It's as if my voice is nowhere to be found. I move toward her, but though I should be getting closer to her, the distance between us grows. It is then that I can hear Laura muttering to herself while she's writing, but I can't make out the words.

Out of the corner of my eye, I see the child move, so I direct my attention to her.

Although she has turned her face toward me, it is still hidden. The words she utters make me want to cry. "You can't save us."

Desperation takes hold of my entire being. I need to reach them. But suddenly, a thick fog flows into the room, making it difficult to see two inches in front of me, let alone the little girl and Laura, who are also in the room. Panic rises as I try to scream, to warn Laura and the little girl, but I still can't speak.

Before I can react, I find myself gasping as I sit up in bed, drenched in sweat.

My heart slams in my chest as I recall the images of my dream. I won't be able to shake that nightmare for a while.

My breaths are labored, but gradually, they even out, and I can focus on the silence that surrounds me. It was just a nightmare, and I'm okay.

I rub my temples in an attempt to ease the headache that is forming. After my talk with Abigail and how much my thoughts spiraled, I'm not surprised that I had a nightmare. It feels as if a boulder dropped on me twice due to having Laura's disappearance and my own trauma wrapped up into one fucked-up dream.

Apparently, my demons didn't sleep either.

I lie back down in the bed and stare at the ceiling. Listening to another voice memo from Laura would probably be the smart thing to do, but I can't seem to force myself to do it.

Instead, I sink farther into the bed and force myself to fall back to sleep in hopes that this time, my demons won't win.

THE SOUND of my ringtone plays in my head, and it takes me a second to realize that it isn't a part of any dream that I'm having. I force my eyes open, my mind still reeling from the nightmare I had hours ago. I reach over and snatch my phone from the nightstand.

> Luke: Hey, would you be up for having dinner at my place? I'll pull out all the stops. Tomorrow evening at seven?

The message from Luke is a welcome distraction after what already seems like the beginning of a pretty bad day.

Part of me knows I should be wary about being alone with Luke because I don't know him. But for some reason, I can't resist. I start typing back to him before I can stop myself.

> Me: I like this plan. Are you going to cook dinner or order out?

> Luke: Cook it all myself. Then maybe we can hit Harbor's Edge for drinks and more conversation if you're up for it.

If I didn't already wish for this day to end quickly, I do now.

> Me: I like that a lot.

> Luke: Excellent. Any food allergies/restrictions/dislikes I should know about?

A smirk plays on my lips before I realize it. I appreciate how thorough he's being.

> Me: No. I'm looking forward to seeing what you cook.

Before he can respond again, I leave my bed and prepare to get ready for today because if I don't do it now, I might just stay in bed all day. Laura needs me and that is what matters above all else.

The time it takes me to shower and get dressed affords me plenty of time to think and try to figure out what I want to do today.

With the newfound information I have, I think it's best that I go back and look through Laura's office. If that is where she spent most of her time, there has to be something I missed about why she was afraid.

That is unless Elliott got rid of any evidence pointing to him.

I open the bedroom door and step out into the hallway. There isn't anyone there, as usual, and I quickly make my way to Laura's office. This time I close the door behind me, hoping that will keep anyone from sneaking up on me.

"What secrets have you been keeping, Laura?" I murmur to myself as I scan the room in hopes of finding something that I missed.

I begin sifting through Laura's desk drawers, skimming papers that were thrown in there. When that turns up empty, I find myself looking through a couple of cardboard boxes that she had in the room, but they don't contain anything worth noting either.

I walk over to her bookshelf to see if she has any books

that look like they might be related to Harrow Isle or the people that inhabit it. My eyes drift down to where I found the picture frame earlier that contained the photo of Laura and me from when we were in college.

I spy an older-looking journal, its leather binding worn and a little frayed around the edges. I pull it out and notice that it feels heavy in my hands. I trace the embossed design on its cover, a series of intertwined circles that form a *B*.

I open it, taking care not to rip any of the pages as they seem very delicate. The pages are yellow with age, and the ink is somewhat faded. The script is rough and doesn't match Laura's handwriting based on some of the notes I saw on her desk. I begin to skim through the book, interested in what it might contain and hoping to discover who it belongs to.

As I flip the pages, a folded piece of paper slips out, landing on the floor. I recognize Laura's writing this time. The note says,

There's a darker connection between Harrow Isle's history and the Bennetts. There's no way this is all by chance. And then, more cryptically, The more I learn, the more I fear for my life.

Suddenly, it clicks. The placement of this journal, hidden behind what would have been the picture frame if it hadn't ended up in the guest room, was on purpose. It's almost as if she wanted me to find it. The likelihood of me picking up that frame with our picture in it was high. Did Laura leave this trail along with the voice memos for me on purpose?

Clutching the journal and Laura's note, I feel the pieces

are coming together even though the whole picture is still a blurry mess.

It is then that I realize I am missing the thing that has been my constant companion since I've been here, Laura's phone. It is back in my purse.

My pulse races as I sprint back to my room. It doesn't even occur to me to look around to see if anyone is out in the hallway before I dart out of the room. If she documented anything that might serve as a guide through this journal, it might be there.

I snatch it from my bag and run back to Laura's office. I barely take the time to close the door before I'm back at her desk and listening to the voice memos.

Soon I hear Laura's voice playing from the device. The first couple of voice memos are about how she still felt isolated on Harrow Isle. But it isn't until I start listening to the third voice memo that I straighten my body. I note that this memo is from three months ago.

"So, I've been digging more into Harrow Isle's past, and the things I'm uncovering are kind of scary. I stumbled upon this old journal in the library downstairs. I can barely believe the things written in there. The things that they've done... I'm afraid to say them out loud. I can't shake this paranoia that someone's watching or following me. I'm jumpy as hell, and maybe I have no reason to be because of how old this book is. But I don't know. I just don't know what to think. I love Elliott, I truly do, but should I bring this up to him? I don't know. This journal, I can't stop thinking about it. Whoever is listening to this, something's probably happened to me. Please don't stop looking. I'm convinced there's something."

The voice memo stops, and I turn my attention to the journal, looking for any signs of where she might have left more notes. If she is confirming that the Bennetts have kidnapped people and who knows what else to maintain their status on this island...I don't even know what to think. I lower the volume on her phone and replay the voice memo for myself once more.

At least that's what I'm trying to do when I hear footsteps approaching.

Instinctively, I shove the journal beneath some scattered papers. The doorknob turns. Trying to hide my panic, I silence Laura midsentence.

The door opens a crack. Elliott's eyes meet mine. There's an intensity in his gaze that wasn't there before. I mentally try to prepare myself for what might be about to come. "What are you doing here, Quinn?" he asks.

"Going over her office once more to see if I missed anything. You said I could come in here," I say, struggling to keep my voice steady. Thoughts of Abigail's cryptic warnings about the Bennetts are blaring like alarms in my head.

His eyes narrow and they stay on me. "Have you found anything interesting?"

Biting back the urge to confront him, I decide to take a different approach. Maybe appealing to the danger that she might be in will work to my advantage. "Not much yet. Are we sure that she just disappeared? It's been days now, and we aren't any closer to finding her."

Elliott steps farther into the room and closes the door behind him. I don't like this one bit. "I don't think she's dead."

That makes me do a double take. "I hope she's not, but we don't know that for sure."

"I do know that for sure."

I raise an eyebrow at him, shoving aside my discomfort with being alone with him. "Explain, please."

"We would have heard about it by now. People always want to get paid and if they had her, I'm sure someone would have come forth. Hell, I'm starting to wonder if she didn't just decide to take off back to New York City as a way to clear her head, and she'll show up back here in a few days. Maybe that's wishful thinking on my part."

I'm convinced that no one who lives here can give me a straight answer.

"On one hand, Laura has always been unpredictable, at least since she and I started dating," he says. "But I do know that she wouldn't just vanish without a word. Not to me. Not like this."

I challenge him, confused about what he is trying to say. "So you don't know for sure what might have happened then."

He moves a step closer, circling around the desk, his fingers brushing over the papers strewn about. I'm concerned that he'll see the journal that I've barely hidden and all the while, I'm looking around the room to see if there is something I can use as a weapon. "Laura and I have been through a lot. Highs and lows. She's passionate and dedicated to the things she cares about. Sometimes overly so." His stare holds mine, issuing an unspoken challenge. "But she has secrets, Quinn, just like everyone else."

Feeling trapped, I force myself to stand my ground. "Maybe if she had felt she could trust the people around her, she wouldn't have kept secrets. Maybe she would still be here right now." It's a bold move, one that I'm not entirely proud of. I know that I'm shifting the blame slightly to him, indicating that he might be a part of the problem.

For a fleeting moment, I think I see a flash of hurt in his eyes, but it's quickly thrown behind a mask. "Be careful with making assumptions, Quinn. They can be more dangerous than the lies people throw around."

Silence fills the room. We stare at each other, daring the other person to say another word.

"I would also be careful about assuming that spending time with Luke is the right thing to do," he finally says, breaking the silence. There's an edge to his tone and I don't like it.

Cautiously, I respond, "Luke has nothing to do with this."

He chuckles, but there's no warmth in it. "The Hartleys and the Bennetts have been at odds for years. Just be wary of who you trust." He tilts his head, studying me. "Especially when you don't know if he has anything to do with my wife's disappearance."

Without another word, he strides toward the door and away from me. He reaches for the doorknob, and there's a brief pause, but soon he's pulling the door to him, crossing the threshold, and closing the door behind him.

And for the first time in what feels like hours, I can breathe freely.

15

QUINN

As I drive toward the address that Luke sent me, I take a quick glance at the sun as it dips lower in the sky. The fading light seems to mirror my own mixed emotions. I'm excited about my evening with Luke, but my concern about Laura and my run-in with Elliott are still at the forefront of my mind.

There is a sudden shift in the state of the homes on this side of Harrow Isle from the side closer to the Bennett estate. The houses here are well kept and welcoming, versus what I'd seen when driving to and from Laura and Elliott's home. I wonder what the cause of the division was.

It takes me a few more minutes, but soon I'm pulling the car to a stop in front of Luke's place. It's a beautiful coastal cottage. It's exactly what I would imagine if I was told I would be staying on an island in the Pacific Northwest.

I take a deep breath as I exit the car, calming my nerves about seeing Luke in a more intimate setting again. I walk up to the front door and knock, waiting for Luke to answer. When the door swings open to Luke standing there with a welcoming smile, I can't help but grin. He gives me a hug before letting me inside. I'm happy that I read the vibes of this date right and that we both decided to dress in jeans and sweaters this evening.

"Hey," he says softly. "Come on in."

"Thanks," I reply, stepping into what, from the outside, looks like a warm and inviting home. I quickly confirm that the inside is too.

The scent of woodsmoke coming from the fireplace is the first thing I smell. The fire is welcome, given how cold it is outside. It is easy for me to see the fireplace because the entrance opens up to a living room where the wooden floorboards softly creak beneath my feet. I glance at the fireplace and am grateful for the heat that is coming from it.

I can't help but smile at the homely touches scattered throughout the space. Nautical maps of Harrow Isle and a painting of a ship over the fireplace make sense for a person who is in love with the sea and the island they live on.

I can see what looks like a nice-sized kitchen and the dining room area that is right next to it. The dining table has two wineglasses and a bottle of wine on it. There are also candles on the table, adding to the romantic vibes. I'm immediately struck by the cozy ambience that this place has and how much of a stark contrast it is to the darkness of the Bennett estate.

After he closes the door behind me, his eyes meet mine, and it feels as if a burden has been lifted, even if it's only for a little while.

As I walk farther into the house, I start to smell something that I think is tomatoes.

"Can I grab your coat?" Luke asks.

I nod quickly and hand it over to him. Once he puts it up, he turns to me and holds out his hand. Once my hand is in his, we make our way over to his dining room table.

By the time I'm seated, Luke is pouring a glass of wine for me and pouring some for himself.

"Do you need help with anything?" I ask as I take a sip of wine.

"Nope. I have everything handled." With that, he walks into the kitchen.

I hear some closing and opening of doors before he walks back toward me. The scent of tomatoes fills the air as Luke brings a steaming baking dish to the table, setting it down carefully. The flickering candlelight casts a warm glow on his face, accentuating the strong lines of his jaw and the intensity that I find in his eyes.

"Made lasagna," he says with a hint of pride. "Hope you like it."

"It smells amazing," I reply, my stomach growling in anticipation for what I know will be a delicious meal. He sits down across from me and our feet brush against one another as he settles down.

Once we take a few bites of our food, Luke is the first to speak. "How is everything going with you? Have you discovered anything more about Laura's disappearance?"

I swirl the wine in my glass for a moment, collecting my thoughts before taking a sip. The rich flavor complements the hearty meal, and the drink gives me an opportunity to think before I answer Luke's question.

"If I'm being honest, there's still a lot I'm trying to piece together. I guess if I had to summarize everything, I don't think this was a case of her simply walking away on her own accord."

I pause because I'm waiting to see what his reaction is. If he's involved, this might make this moment... interesting.

Luke's face is filled with concern, but his expression doesn't give away any sign of guilt. "That's frustrating, given how long she's been gone. If there's any way I can help, let me know."

My lips form a faint smile. I appreciate that he is willing to give his support. "I might have a few questions about the history of this island and who might want to keep... certain things buried."

"The Bennetts," Luke says immediately. "And I'm not just saying that because our families hate each other."

"What do you mean?" If Luke and Abigail's stories are similar, I'll be leaning harder into who I think is responsible for all of this.

Luke takes a sip of his wine as a thoughtful look crosses his face. "The Bennetts are both influential and controversial, and they are determined to always be the family that has all the power. Whether it's being mayor of the island or getting a set of kickbacks that are very beneficial to their bottom lines when it comes to the various businesses they are in."

I nod, pushing my food around with my fork. "I've heard something about this before," I say, recalling my conversation with Abigail.

He chuckles softly, though there's no humor in it. "Have you also heard about the folklore regarding them?"

"No," I answer slowly, wondering where this could be going.

"According to stories that have been passed down for

generations, the Bennetts pissed off enough people that someone somewhere has cursed them. There are some circumstances that would make one wonder if that was the case..."

I look up from my plate, meeting his gaze. "And Laura, being married to Elliott, would be associated with this *curse*?"

Luke shrugs. "I mean, she's technically a Bennett. When it was first reported that she was missing, I thought she left Elliott. Apparently, I wasn't the only one in town who thought that either."

"Interesting..." is all I can think to say.

We fall into a somewhat strange silence because we are both lost in our thoughts. With his version of stories, Luke has confirmed what Abigail was hinting to me, that I definitely need to be careful around Elliott. Maybe staying in town wouldn't be such a bad idea.

Then again, who knows what secrets are actually on the Bennett estate that I would have easy access to if I stayed there? After a bit, I decide to change the topic. "This dish is amazing, by the way. You're a fantastic cook."

He grins, the earlier tension replaced, and the mood shifts to us being more relaxed. "There are a lot of things you don't know about me, Quinn. Cooking happens to be one of my favorite pastimes."

I laugh, grateful for the change. "Well, consider me impressed. If you ever want to change your bar into a restaurant, you'll be successful."

That makes Luke laugh. I knew building and running a restaurant was much more complicated than I'd indicated, but I was happy to continue to ease the tension.

With dinner behind us, we stand up and move our used

dishes to the sink. Luke leads me into his living room toward the warm glow of the fireplace. The flames dance and crackle and it is poetic in a way. The room is full of dark wood and furniture, and the air is thick with the scent of leather from well-worn books lining the shelves. Once again, the definition of cozy fits this house to a tee.

We sit down on the couch, and I struggle to find the words that I want to say. It's weird because I'm usually the person that people go to for answers, and I still have none.

"Luke," I begin tentatively, "I want to thank you for all of this and for sharing some of the information you have on the Bennetts. It is helpful, more than you know."

He turns to me and gently grabs my hand. "You don't have to thank me, Quinn. I want to help–not just because of Laura, but because I care about you too."

His words send a flurry of butterflies through my stomach. "You know, I've spent most of my life building walls around myself, trying to keep others at arm's length. But I enjoy talking to you. This also might be superheavy for a second date."

"Everyone has their reasons for closing themselves off," he says softly as he squeezes my hand. "Is that why you became a therapist?" he asks. "To help others heal from their own pain?"

"Partly," I admit, searching for the right words. "But it's also because I've been running from my own demons for so long. Helping others is a way for me to confront them, or so I like to think."

I'm grateful for and hate the warmth of Luke's hand on mine because I feel secure with him in spite of everything that's going on.

"There's been something I've wanted to do since you first walked into my bar."

"Oh yeah?"

When he leans closer to me, I know what's coming and I won't deny that I can't wait.

I watch as he closes the distance between us. Our lips meet slowly at first, giving in to a soft exploration of each other. Soon the kiss deepens, fueled by the urgency of our situation and the pent-up emotions. His hands find my face while mine settle on his chest, feeling the rapid beat of his heart.

It feels like time has stopped. In this moment, it's just the two of us seeking comfort and understanding from one another.

As we pull apart, our foreheads rest together, and we take a second to catch our breath. I wish that all the rest of the things that we have to take care of would fade away and we could stay this way forever.

"Let's get out of here," Luke suggests. "I promised to take you to The Harbor's Edge."

"Sure," I reply. "It probably would have made more sense for you to pick me up from where I'm staying."

"It's probably best for me to not be on Bennett property. We can drive over separately if you want. Or I can drive us and bring you back here to collect your car and drive home after that. Whatever it is that you want to do."

I think about it for a minute before I decide. "I'll ride with you there." It leaves our evening open-ended, and I'm perfectly okay with that. By the look on his face, I think I've made the right decision.

We put our coats on and soon find ourselves stepping out

into the brisk air. It doesn't take us too long to get to Luke's bar and as soon as we walk in, everyone is walking up to Luke to greet him. It's interesting to see how everyone treats Luke when he's not behind the bar.

"Come on," Luke says, guiding me toward a secluded corner booth.

As we settle into our seats, I realize that even in this different setting, the intimacy between us remains the same. We settle on getting a beer and a glass of water each before we start talking again.

Our conversation flows like we've known each other our whole lives. My laughter mingles with Luke's as he finishes telling a hilarious story from his time in the military.

"That is one of the most absurd stories I've ever heard," I say, shaking my head in amusement. "It's hard to imagine you getting into that kind of trouble."

"Believe it or not, I wasn't always this responsible, upstanding citizen you see before you," he teases, a smirk playing at the corners of his mouth. "What about you?"

As I'm about to speak, I notice out of the corner of my eye that someone else has just walked into the bar. Joanna, Laura's best friend, waltzes in, exuding an air of confidence that commands attention. Her long hair is swept back into a loose ponytail, and her eyes are darting around the room as if she is looking for something or someone.

"Quinn," Luke murmurs, following my gaze. "What's up?"

"Joanna just walked in," I reply, watching as she greets a few people before her gaze lands on our table. The smile that graces her face is warm but tight.

"Quinn, Luke," she says. "I hope you're enjoying your evening."

"I think we are." I glance at Luke before I look back at Joanna.

"Good, good." She nods. "Actually, I was hoping that you and I could get together soon. To talk about Laura."

That gets my attention. "Sure."

Joanna looks down at the ground and says, "I'll stop by Elliott's either tomorrow or the next day and we can talk."

"Okay." All of this is strange, but I am not about to say something and mess this up.

"I don't want to take up too much of your time, so I'll let you two go."

Joanna doesn't wait for me to respond before she leaves. I'm left staring at her as she walks away, but my eyes aren't staring at her back.

They're staring at her purse, which currently has what looks like a red piece of fabric poking out of it.

16

QUINN

The light in the bathroom is way too bright. Or maybe it is the fact that I got back to my room just before the sun was coming up. I slept in. But it isn't enough, I need more sleep, but apparently, I'm not getting any more. I throw on a hoodie over my pajamas and walk into the hallway.

"Quinn?"

I freeze in place, confusion written all over my face. Why is Mrs. Fleming calling me?

As I walk down the stairs, I see Mrs. Fleming, and next to her is a bouquet of mysterious black roses resting on a small table in the foyer. I approach the roses and notice that there is no card or note attached to them.

"Who are these for?" I ask, not sure if I'm directing my question to Mrs. Fleming. I reach out and brush my fingertips against the soft petals. Who would send someone black roses? And why not leave a note to tell the person who sent them?

"I'm not sure. I assumed they were for you," Mrs. Fleming says as she studies the flowers.

"I don't think I've ever seen flowers like this before."

"Me either. In all my years working here, never." Mrs. Fleming shakes her head and I notice that she looks worried. "Black roses aren't a good sign."

I know that, but I'm curious about what she has to say. "Why? What do they mean?"

Mrs. Fleming hesitates, her gaze drifting around the room and landing anywhere but on me or the flowers. "They can mean many things, but here, they are often seen as a bad omen. A warning of sorts."

I let out a deep breath. "A warning against what?"

"It could be a multitude of things."

The silence that passes between us makes me wonder if we are thinking the same thing. The roses only came when I started snooping around.

"Have you told Elliott about this?" I ask.

Mrs. Fleming glances toward the entrance, her face tightening. "He is in a meeting right now, but should be out soon."

Before I can respond, the doorbell rings and both Mrs. Fleming and I share a look with one another. Apparently neither one of us is expecting anyone. She walks to the door and opens it. I'm surprised to see Joanna, and in her hand is a vibrant red scarf. Did it belong to Laura?

"I found this in my home," she says as her eyes dart between the roses and the scarf. "I think she might have left it at my house."

That is strange because Elliott told me that the last time he saw Laura, she had the scarf on.

"When was Laura last at your house?"

Joanna hesitates for just a moment, her gaze shifting to mine before she speaks. "She visited a few days before she disappeared. She wanted to discuss something with me."

"What?" I ask, my voice sharper than I intend. How could she wait to give this information? Why is she lying if Laura had the scarf on when she went missing?

Joanna looks like she's debating with herself about what she should and shouldn't say. "It was private. I promised her I wouldn't discuss it. But given everything, I'm starting to think maybe I should."

"Does it have anything to do with the scarf? What did Laura want to talk about?"

Before she can say another word, Elliott walks into the foyer and I can see that he is taking in the scene before him. His gaze lands on Joanna and it stays there for a second too long. When he notices the scarf, I swear I see a flicker of recognition flash across his face.

Or is it fear?

"Joanna, what are you doing here?" he asks.

"Good morning," Joanna replies evenly, her grip on the scarf showcasing her nerves. "I came to return this because I found it at my place."

"Is that so?" Elliott's gaze remains fixed on the scarf.

"Yes, you, of all people, should know that I wouldn't lie about this."

Elliott's eyes linger on the scarf for another moment before meeting Joanna's. Mrs. Fleming and I exchange a glance as the questions about what the hell is going on here spring into my mind. I don't want to draw assumptions, but a million and one of them are flying through my mind right now.

"I didn't imply that you'd lie," Elliott says as he crosses his arms and his whole posture turns rigid.

Joanna takes a deep breath, attempting to maintain her composure. "The look on your face said it all."

Elliott rolls his eyes. "You always did have a vivid imagination."

Joanna stiffens. "I think this is enough of this line of questioning. Our focus should be on Laura."

"Don't you think I know that?" Elliott replies, and his voice is as cold as the wind that is blowing outside this very house.

Joanna nods in agreement, her fingers still white-knuckled around the scarf. "It is pointless for me to have this argument with you. I brought the scarf over and that is all the information I have."

In reality, I know it is the only information she is willing to give because she admitted that Laura came over to her house to talk about a private matter.

I can't help but speak up. "And I appreciate that, Joanna. Everything that we find related to Laura counts." I try to do my best to ease the tension, but I'm not sure I am successful.

Joanna hands the scarf to Elliott before clearing her throat. "I've done what I came here to do. Now, if you'll excuse me." She gives a nod to Mrs. Fleming and a small glance in my direction before practically running out of the Bennett home.

After Joanna shuts the door behind her, I look at Elliott, who is staring down at the scarf in his hand. He gently shakes his head and tosses the scarf onto the banister before he, too, walks away.

Mrs. Fleming and I are silent for a beat before she speaks. "What should I do with these roses?"

"Find out if the police can figure out who sent them? We can also try calling the florist to see if they would be willing to identify who it was."

Mrs. Fleming nods. "I'll put them in the kitchen." With that, she walks up to the bouquet, grabs the vase, and leaves the room.

I watch as Mrs. Fleming walks down the hall and when I know she's not coming back, I snatch the scarf off the banister and head up to my room.

As I'm playing with the scarf, I find myself trying to figure out what the hell was up with what I just witnessed.

Elliott and Joanna's exchange wasn't just about a misplaced scarf. There was something much deeper at play. The way their eyes locked, the guarded body language. It was as if they were having two conversations simultaneously, and I only had the privilege of understanding one.

Elliott's defensiveness was apparent, but it didn't make any sense. And Joanna was clearly holding something back.

I might have been able to find out what it was if Elliott hadn't interrupted us.

I sit on the edge of my bed and as I'm replaying the exchange in my mind, I absently play with the vibrant red scarf Joanna brought over.

Suddenly, my fingers stop moving. I feel an unexpected bump in the fabric. Examining it closer, I find a hidden compartment sewn into the scarf. Pulling the stitched flap back, I find a small, folded piece of paper that I take out of its hiding spot.

With trembling fingers, I unfold it and instantly recognize Laura's handwriting.

Trust no one in the Bennett mansion.

A chill runs down my spine. What had Laura stumbled upon? What did she fear? Or maybe the better question is, who did she fear?

Suddenly, a muffled sound grabs my attention. It takes me a second to realize that it is the sound of raised voices. I move cautiously to the window in this room, and I scan the area until I find the source. Below, I see Joanna and Elliott talking to one another. Based on how tense they look, I can tell that the conversation isn't a happy one. Hell, I would be willing to bet that they are having an argument.

There is a chance that this will fall flat, but I need to try. I grab the red scarf and sprint out of the room, down the stairs and head to the back of the house so that I might have a chance of hearing what they are talking about. I hide behind a bush and pray that I won't make a sound that will give me away.

"You just don't get it, do you?" It's easy to spot the frustration in Joanna's voice. "I've given you everything, every part of me. Whether Laura returns or not, I want you by my side. You know that it was always supposed to be you and me."

There's a weighted pause before Elliott replies, sounding exhausted, "Joanna, this isn't about just my feelings. It's about choices, about the man I want to be. Regardless of where Laura is."

Straining to catch every word, I press closer to the bush, barely daring to breathe.

Joanna's voice softens, dripping with anguish. "Choose me then. Choose us."

Another heavy silence. Then he says, "I want to make amends with Laura, give our marriage a second chance. Whatever this is between you and me was a mistake."

Joanna's voice cracks, "So you're ending this? Just like that?"

I watch as she throws up her hands and briskly walks to her car, ending the conversation. Elliott is left alone, staring at her. Without warning, his gaze drifts upward as if he is looking in the direction of my bedroom, but I'm not there. Then he turns and walks away, disappearing into the mansion.

Could Joanna have kidnapped Laura? That doesn't seem too far-fetch now if I am being honest with myself. But it doesn't explain the warning hidden in this scarf. Is it meant for me? For Joanna? Or someone else?

I glance down at the red scarf and the note it carries. Every time I turn, it seems as if the more information I untangle about Laura's disappearance, the more complex everything gets.

17

QUINN

The grandfather clock in the hallway chimes as I walk past it, marking the passing of another hour as its tone echoes through the spacious corridors of the Bennett mansion. It's only been an hour since I found that chilling note hidden within the red scarf.

Everything in here reminds me of Laura's warning for whoever found the note:

Trust no one in the Bennett mansion.

Drawing in a deep breath, I try to push away the paranoia that is bubbling in my chest. But it's hard being in a house that you've been warned against. Each creak and sigh from this home only amplifies my feeling of being watched or worse.

Hearing the faint footsteps of someone nearby, my steps slow as I find Mr. Gregory carefully adjusting a portrait of a beautiful landscape that is hanging on a wall in the living room. Throughout my time here, I've had limited interactions with him, but I've seen him enough times to know that he is everywhere all of the time. He's been serving as the Bennetts' butler for years, and maybe he might have some of the answers I'm looking for. After all, if anyone knows the intricacies of this home and the Bennett family, it's Mr. Gregory. And right now, I need every clue I can get. He moves on to another portrait, this one of a couple.

I take a moment to study the painting before I say a word. "Mr. Gregory," I begin, trying to sound as if everything is fine. "That's a beautiful portrait."

He jumps slightly, his fingers freezing in the air, but quickly composes himself. His expression quickly veers between being nervous and being unreadable. It is slightly comforting that at least I'm not the only one who is panicky. "It is, isn't it? It's a painting of Theodore Bennett and his wife, Hazel."

"Interesting." I'm intrigued by this because of the old photo Abigail showed me. There is something else there that I'm missing, but I'm not sure what conclusion I should reach. "Elliott looks a lot like him."

He stares at the picture as if he just noticed something new about it. "He does, as does Mr. Bennett's father."

"Where are Elliott's parents anyway?"

"They passed away a few years back. Terrible car accident."

That is fascinating to me, given the things I know about the Bennetts being cursed. However, that isn't the reason I was talking to Mr. Gregory.

Taking a deep breath, I dive into the question I've been itching to ask. "Around the time Laura disappeared, did you notice anything strange? Any changes in her behavior or unexpected events?"

He stiffens at my inquiry as his eyes narrow slightly. "Strange occurrences? No, nothing comes to mind, although she did have a flair for... Never mind. One day she was here, and the next day she was gone."

I watch as his eyes land on me before he quickly turns back to the portrait. It's only for a second, but it doesn't sit right with me.

"Are you sure, Mr. Gregory? What did she have a flair for?" I press, trying to maintain a neutral demeanor. "It's just that Laura's disappearance is so strange, and as someone who was around her so often because of how long you've worked here, I thought you might have noticed something."

His lips tighten into a thin line, and he shifts his weight from one foot to the other. "Ms. Pierce, I assure you, if there was anything out of the ordinary, I would have said something to Mr. Bennett. As I said before, I didn't see anything that was strange."

"But what did she have a flair for?"

His eyes shift behind his glasses and I'm sure he's weighing whether he wants to tell me or not. With a sigh, he says, "Being dramatic. Please don't tell Mr. Bennett I said that."

"Thank you for your honesty, Mr. Gregory. I know it's been difficult for everyone."

"Indeed, it has," he replies. "We're all hoping for Laura's safe return. If you'll excuse me, I have duties to attend to."

I hesitate for a moment, watching Mr. Gregory's retreating figure before the words fall out of my mouth. "Mr. Gregory, wait."

He turns to face me, his expression unreadable. "Is there something else?" The clipped formality in his tone reveals his impatience when it comes to talking to me.

"I noticed that a picture of Laura and me from our college days was moved from her office to my room. Do you know anything about that?"

He hesitates for a moment before responding, "Ah, yes. I placed it there myself. I thought it might serve as some comfort to you during your stay."

"Comfort?" I repeat, narrowing my eyes at his choice of words. Why would he think a photo of a missing person would bring me comfort?

"Perhaps comfort was not the right word," he admits, looking slightly embarrassed. "But I thought it might remind you of happier times and make your room feel homier."

"Thank you, Mr. Gregory," I say, but I don't mean it.

"If you'll excuse me, Ms. Pierce." With that, he leaves the room, and I'm left alone with my thoughts.

I wait a moment before I leave the living room and continue down the hallway. Then I hear someone speaking.

"I don't know what to do—" Elliott's voice catches in his throat, and I can almost imagine the panic etched across his face. "This can't go on anymore."

As I strain to hear more, my heart pounds loudly in my ears, drowning out his words. Who is Elliott talking to? And what is he talking about?

"I said that this is over. This is the end."

I wish that I could hear what the person on the other end of the line is saying, but I can't help but wonder if it is Joanna. Though the conversation is too muffled to make out specific details, the urgency in Elliott's voice has me on high alert.

"Listen, I need to go."

At those words, I slowly back away, hoping that nothing will creak and give my hiding spot away.

When I reach the stairs, I increase my pace and let out a deep breath when I return to my room. My fingers tremble as I lock the door behind me, the metallic click sounds like a resounding thud through the air. Everything that has happened today has urged me to act.

I grab the wooden chair that is in front of the desk in this room. I place it under the doorknob and take a step back. It won't stop anyone from getting in, but at least it will alert me that someone is attempting to come in.

18

LAURA

Two Weeks before Her Disappearance

I can't help but smile as I look at my husband. His eyes are closed, his breathing slow and steady. For a moment, it feels like nothing in the world exists outside of our bedroom. My heart swells as I watch him sleep, wondering how I got to be so lucky to have him in my life. Or so I continue to tell myself even when we are having our issues.

"Good morning," I whisper, brushing a stray lock of hair from his forehead.

Elliott stirs slightly, his eyelids fluttering open to reveal those dark-brown eyes I fell in love with all those years ago. "Morning," he murmurs, his voice still thick with sleep.

"Breakfast?"

"Sounds good," he replies, shifting away from me as he rises from the bed.

I miss his warmth immediately.

Elliott has always been my rock, but lately, something

feels off. However, I'm determined to make the best of what I want to be a quiet morning.

As we sit down for breakfast, Mrs. Fleming serves him scrambled eggs and toast, just the way he likes them. If I had to describe the mood at the table, I would say there is a storm brewing beneath the surface, but I try to keep my emotions in check. I take a deep breath and try to smile, asking, "So, how's work going?"

"Fine. I'm probably going to have to fly to Arizona this week. And how is your fundraiser going?"

"Good," I say, forcing a tight-lipped smile. This is the first time he's asked me about it, and I've been working on things for it for months. "Joanna's been such a great help."

I didn't mean to mention Joanna, but her name just slipped out.

This time, he looks up at me. "How is she doing anyway?"

"She's well. Busy as usual."

I pause to think about what I want to say next, and Elliott does nothing to fill in the void. He doesn't ask me more about what I'm doing or what I'm reading. The façade that I put up quickly crumbles the more I think about it and the longer the silence passes between us.

"You know," I start. "I probably see her more nowadays than I see you." The words escape before I can stop them. The tension between Elliott and I lights up as if a firecracker has gone off.

Elliott's eyes search mine before narrowing. "What's that supposed to mean?"

"Nothing." I sigh, pushing my plate away from me, having suddenly lost my appetite. "It's just that you've been distant lately."

He scoffs, avoiding my gaze. "I've been busy, Laura."

"Too busy for your wife?" I snap, surprising even myself.

Elliott rolls his eyes. "I don't have time for this."

"Of course you don't. You don't have time for anything that relates to me anymore!" I exclaim, my heart pounding in my chest.

"I'm not doing this with you right now." Elliott stands up abruptly. He leaves the table without another word, leaving me to sit in the wreckage of our crumbling relationship.

As I watch him go, I can't help but wonder how we got here. How did the man who once made me feel like I was the center of his universe become a stranger to me?

When the door slams shut, I jump. The sound echoes throughout the mansion. It is just another example of how alone I am here. I sit in silence for a moment as my eyes wander to one of the many grandfather clocks we have in this home. I would be willing to swear that its ticking is growing louder with each second that passes. It feels as if time is slowly starting to run out on us.

I'm grateful that none of the staff comes in to check on what might have happened between Elliott and me. I rise from my chair and head upstairs, determined to hide away for the time being.

I decide to go up to our bedroom and get my phone. I want to record another voice memo because that seems to help me process my thoughts. But it isn't on my nightstand. I check the floor and notice something under our bed. I reach down to pick it up. It's a necklace—a delicate silver chain adorned with a single opal pendant. While it is a beautiful piece, there is something even more obvious about it.

It's not mine.

A pit forms in my stomach as the implications of its presence in our room and the current state of my relationship begins to dawn on me.

"Are you really that naive?" I say out loud to myself. "Do you honestly believe he's been faithful all this time?"

I shake my head, willing the thoughts away. No, I can't let myself think like that. Elliott loves me, doesn't he? We have our issues, but so does everyone else. He wouldn't betray me like this. However, the evidence sits right there in my hand.

I stare at the necklace for a moment longer, my heart pounding even harder than it was when we were arguing just moments before. I know what I have to do, but the fear of what I might uncover threatens to consume me whole. But I know it's something that I must do.

I pace in my bedroom, overthinking every potential explanation for the necklace on the floor near my bed. I only briefly stop in order to get dressed for the day, but even then, I still think about the necklace.

Now that I have it in my hand once more, the weight of the necklace seems to grow heavier by the second. I've been thinking about what I should do for long enough and have finally come to a decision. With a deep breath, I pocket the delicate chain and make my way downstairs to talk to Elliott. I find him in his office, staring at some papers on his desk.

"Yes?" he asks as I enter. The remnants of our last argument are still in the air and it's only about to get worse.

I close the door behind me before I turn to face him. "Tell me," I say, trying to keep my voice steady, "who does this belong to?"

I pull the necklace from my pocket, letting it dangle between my fingers. Elliott's gaze flicks to the jewelry, then back to me, his expression unreadable. He hesitates for a fraction of a second before answering, "I have no idea. I've never seen it before."

"Really? Because I found it in our bedroom."

"Maybe it's yours." I can hear the irritation in his tone.

"Cut the bullshit, Elliott," I snap. "You know it isn't mine. Now tell me the truth."

"Fine." He sighs, running a hand through his hair. "It belonged to an ex-girlfriend. I thought I'd gotten rid of it years ago."

"An ex-girlfriend?" I repeat. I want to believe him, but he's already lied about seeing it before. "Why would you keep something like that? How did you get it back if it was a gift from you?"

"She returned it to me after we broke up. I didn't mean to keep it. I'm not sure how it ended up in our room though, because I thought I had it buried in a box with some old things from before we met."

"Or maybe it's not from an ex at all," I argue. "Maybe you bought this for someone more recently."

"You think I'm cheating on you?" he demands, his eyes narrowing. "Laura, you know I would never—"

"Just like you wouldn't lie to me? You just fucking did!" I interrupt, my voice shaking with the force of my emotions.

"I'm not cheating on you."

"Why does it sound like you're lying to me again?"

"Believe what you want, Laura," Elliott snaps, his voice cold and distant.

"I will. Because I know what the truth is."

I toss the necklace so that it lands on his desk just before I storm out of the room. I walk up the stairs and find myself in my office, where I apparently left my phone. I close the door behind me and snatch my phone off my desk, gripping it for dear life.

I pace until I calm myself down enough to where I feel as if I can speak. I quickly find my voice memo app and press the record button.

"My marriage is unraveling at the seams. I think my husband is having an affair. How did it come to this?"

I take a deep breath before I speak again. "It's not just the late nights or him not being interested in me anymore. It's what I've found now. This morning I found a necklace with a silver chain and a single opal pendant on the floor of our bedroom near my side of the bed. It doesn't belong to me and when I asked him about it, he was caught off guard and he lied."

Swallowing hard, I continue. "First, he said he'd never seen it before. But when I pushed, he admitted that it was a gift for an ex-girlfriend. Said she returned it after their breakup. Why would he keep it? Why lie at first?"

Tears prick at my eyes, but I refuse to let them fall. "Who does it belong to? Why hide it? I swear I don't recognize him anymore." I take a deep, steadying breath.

"Maybe it's my own fault," I say. "I was the one who started digging into the Bennetts' family history and trying to uncover the connection to Harrow Isle's history."

"Ever since I became obsessed with it, things between us have been different," I confess, my mind racing as I try to piece together the fragments of my shattered life.

A quiet sob breaks from me, and I wipe away a tear quickly. "All that to say, I don't want to jump to conclusions, but it's obvious something's not right. I can feel it. I just need to know the truth."

I end the memo, my fingers trembling slightly.

For a moment, I sit in silence, staring blankly at the wall straight ahead because I have nothing left. The life I once knew is crumbling, and I'm left grasping for answers in a world shrouded in darkness and deceit.

What am I supposed to do now? How can I face Elliott or the staff, who are probably aiding Elliott in keeping this quiet? These are the people I once trusted with my life, and no one said a word.

"Please," I whisper to the silence in my office, "tell me what to do."

19

QUINN

Normally I would be embracing the fact that I'm sitting in front of a lovely fireplace, but I don't have the opportunity to. I am too busy typing on the keyboard of Laura's laptop. This isn't the first time I've been on her laptop, but tonight, I decided to take a more thorough look to see if there are any hints as to where she could be or what she was doing that might have pissed whoever kidnapped her off enough to come after her. I'm navigating through her personal files, including emails, photos, and articles, as I try to find something that will tell me what happened in the days that led up to her disappearance.

As I dive deeper, a recently accessed folder titled "HI History" catches my eye. It's filled with an assortment of scanned newspaper articles, vintage photographs, and several hastily written notes, some from Laura herself.

One article from a 1980s newspaper headline states: "Unexplained Disappearance Shakes Harrow Isle Once Again." The black-and-white image portrays a solemn-looking group of island residents, their faces etched with concern. This not only further confirms that she had zeroed in on this pattern too, but also that the island has a dark history of people vanishing without a trace.

Another file, a photograph, depicts an old image of a grand ceremony on the island, with a note scribbled at the bottom: "Founding of Harrow Isle."

My heart rate quickens as I stumble upon an email that was never sent. "There's more to this place than meets the eye. There are so many mysteries that I could spend weeks trying to unravel and solve every single one. I'm willing to bet that everyone here has at least one dark secret. I can't shake the feeling that I'm being watched, especially after my latest discoveries."

But that is it. There isn't any follow-up or anything but that email in the drafts. I couldn't help but wonder who she was planning on sending it to.

While I've already been trying to be mindful of what I'm doing and who I'm around, especially in this house, it makes me want to raise my guard even more. So far, no one has tried to come into my room with my makeshift alarm system with the chair underneath the doorknob.

When my eyes start to cross, I close Laura's laptop. There is no doubt that I'm done for the night. I stretch my arms above my head as I stand to begin my journey up the stairs to put this back and get ready for bed.

As I'm walking back to Laura's office to put her laptop back in its place, I can hear some rustling inside of Laura's office. I pause, straining my ears to detect any sounds or movements. It takes me a second before I hear a conversation that is happening so low that if I hadn't stopped, I know I would have missed it. I take a couple of steps, hoping I'll avoid the floorboards that will creak under my weight so that I won't alert whoever is speaking.

I glance into the room and see Mrs. Fleming and Mr. Gregory. I move back so that they can't see me eavesdropping.

"What are you up to?" Mrs. Fleming asks.

"What do you mean what am I up to? I'm just doing my job."

"I've known you for years. But these past few weeks, you've been acting strange. More nervous than usual. I was willing to let it go, but now it's become too much. What is going on?"

"You're reading too much into things."

"I know you better than you think I do," says Mrs. Fleming. "I want to help you if I can."

"All you need to know is that I've made choices. Choices that promise me a way out of certain issues in due time."

"But at what cost?"

I wish I could see their faces, and read their facial expressions and body language.

"The money," he confesses in a near whisper, "it's enough to change everything. It's enough to change my life."

"But what did you do?"

I hear someone take a step and then Mr. Gregory says, "Promise me you'll stay out of it, Mrs. Fleming. The less you know, the safer you'll be."

Drawing back from the doorway, my heart races. What is Mr. Gregory involved in?

20

QUINN

As I take a sip from my coffee, it feels as if it wraps around me like a medium-sized embrace. The warmth that I'm getting from this cup of happiness is everything I need in this moment. It feels as if it's seeping into every pore as I try to focus on the voice memo playing through my earbuds.

"My marriage is unraveling at the seams. I think my husband is having an affair. How did it come to this?"

I tap the phone screen to pause the memo, rubbing my temples in frustration. My eyes shift to the emails currently sitting unanswered in my inbox, a constant reminder of the work I left behind in Seattle. I've decided that it's best for me to stay out of the Bennett mansion as much as possible and that is why I'm sitting in one of the few coffee shops on Harrow Isle.

"Alright," I whisper to myself, forcing my attention back to my inbox. "Let's see what we have here."

As I skim my inbox, I glance toward the entrance, and I

see Joanna stepping inside the coffee shop. I'm beginning to wonder if she's following me.

Joanna seems distracted, with her phone pressed tightly to her ear. She lowers her voice further, but her frustration is clear from the look on her face. I know I shouldn't eavesdrop, but I take my headphones out and I manage to only catch phrases like "not now" and "it's not the right time."

She hangs up, a flash of anger in her eyes before she heads to the counter to place an order. Once she's done, she looks around and I look back down at my laptop.

After what feels like an eternity, I muster the courage to look again. Joanna has taken a seat far from me, her back turned, seemingly engrossed in whatever she's working on. With a deep exhale, I decide it might be best to pack up and leave. The last thing I want is a confrontation, even though this situation is begging for one. It takes me a minute or two to finish my coffee, but as soon as I'm done, I close my laptop and begin to gather my things. Then a shadow looms over my table.

"Quinn." Joanna's voice is smooth but carries an edge of uncertainty. "Hey. Didn't expect to see you here."

I look up, my eyes meeting hers, and suddenly the café's ambient noise fades into the background.

"I was just thinking the same thing," I reply, struggling to keep my voice steady.

Joanna smiles, but I'm not surprised when it doesn't reach her eyes. "Working on something important?" she asks, nodding toward my now-closed laptop.

"Just some work stuff for my practice," I answer. I intentionally don't ask her what she is doing here or how she is doing because I'm hoping to get out of there and that she takes the hint.

Either she doesn't notice what I'm trying to do, or she ignores it. She hesitates for a moment before pulling out the chair opposite me and I fight back a sigh. My eyes look at her face before they land on the necklace she's wearing, and it takes everything in me to not gasp out loud. Silver chain, opal pendant. That can't be a coincidence.

"You seem distracted," Joanna says, disrupting my thoughts. "Is everything okay?"

The directness of her question catches me off guard. "No, but then again, Laura is still missing, so..."

Joanna nods, her fingers lightly touching the necklace. "The more time passes, the more worried I become."

My heart skips a beat. This is it. The moment to address this piece of jewelry that I've been thinking about since I listened to Laura's latest memo. "That's a pretty necklace."

"Thanks a lot. I'm in love with it."

"Is that new?" I ask cautiously, trying to remove any hint of my suspicions.

Joanna smiles. "Yes, actually. Laura gave it to me just before she vanished. She wanted to thank me for helping her with some of the fundraisers she was putting together."

"Really?" I try to steady my breathing, reminding myself that she doesn't know that I know what she is saying is bullshit.

"Yes," Joanna continues, completely unaware of all the thoughts swirling through my mind. "She insisted I take it, said it would bring me luck. I thought I lost it, but I found it recently and have been wearing it ever since, hoping it might, I don't know, maybe bring her back somehow."

"Maybe it will," I say softly, forcing a smile to my lips.

Tears form in Joanna's eyes, and I am not sure if they are real or fake. "I hope so. Laura and I had our differences throughout our friendship, but with everything that has happened it's made me reevaluate a lot."

I raise an eyebrow. "Differences?"

She sighs, looking down at the table, tracing a finger along the grain of the wood. "We both have strong personalities, and sometimes our ideas clashed, and it strained our friendship, but we were always there for one another."

"That happens to the best of us."

"I know," Joanna replies, lifting her gaze to meet mine. "I've been thinking a lot about those times. The laughter, the arguments but in the end, we always made up and things were fine."

I nod slowly, pretending that I am listening to her intently. Part of me wants to press on, dig deeper, call her out about the necklace that I am pretty sure came from Laura's husband and not Laura herself. But another part reminds me of the necessity to be careful.

After a brief silence, I clear my throat. "It's kind of ironic, isn't it? That necklace... Laura believed it would bring luck, and yet we're dealing with her kidnapping..."

A tear falls from Joanna's face, and she says, "Life can be so unpredictable and cruel."

As Joanna's voice trails off, the sudden shrill ring of my phone cuts our somber conversation short. I'm momentarily disoriented, surprised by the sound. Fumbling slightly, I pull it out of my bag, glancing down to see Elliott's name on the screen.

"Sorry, I need to take this," I look at Joanna, who nods

understandingly, wiping away her tears with the back of her hand.

"Go ahead," she says, and it's barely audible.

Pressing the answer button, I lift the phone to my ear. "Hello?"

"Quinn, it's Elliott," he says, but he sounds as if he's trying to catch his breath. "They've found Laura. She's been taken to the hospital."

My heart leaps into my throat, and for a moment, I freeze. The weight of his words sinks in, and I find myself on my feet, already gathering my belongings in frantic haste.

"Which hospital?" Somehow I manage to get the words out, and I'm shocked because the adrenaline is pumping through me.

"Harrow Isle Hospital, but I don't have all the details yet," Elliott's voice cracks. "Please, Quinn, just get here as soon as you can."

"Of course, I'm on my way." Ending the call, I turn to Joanna, my mind racing with a thousand questions. "Laura's been found. She's in the hospital."

"Quinn, that's... amazing." Joanna's eyes widen in disbelief.

"I know. Maybe that necklace you're wearing is good luck."

I hurry out of the coffee shop without waiting for Joanna's response. I run to my car and hope that this soon will be the end of this nightmare.

21

QUINN

After pulling into a parking spot at the Harrow Isle Hospital, I take a moment to try to collect my scattered thoughts. Once I accomplish that task, I step out of the car and make my way inside.

The automatic doors open, and I'm greeted by the scent of antiseptics. The reception area is almost empty, save for a nurse engrossed in paperwork behind the counter. I'm about to approach her when I spot Elliott pacing outside a door farther down the corridor. His face is drawn, eyes red-rimmed, worry coloring his face.

"Elliott?" I say softly, in hopes of not startling him.

He jerks his head up, eyes widening for a second, then narrowing as he tries to place me in this unexpected context. "Quinn? I didn't think you'd get here so quickly."

"I was nearby," I say, which is only half a lie. Thank goodness for GPS and a lead foot. "How is she?"

He swallows hard, avoiding my gaze. "Stable, but she's still been through a lot."

Before I can ask any more questions, Joanna appears at

the end of the hallway. Part of me feels guilty for not offering her a ride, but on the other hand, I'm angry that she would have the audacity to show up here when it's obvious, at least to me, that she is having an affair with Elliott.

She hurries toward us. "Is she okay? Can we see her?" she asks breathlessly.

Elliott nods toward the door. "Not right now, but when they allow visitors, they're letting in family first." Joanna makes a move like she wants to hug Elliott, but Elliott's gaze lands on me and I know he's warning her without saying a word.

"Do we know what happened?" I ask, breaking up whatever moment these two are having. This is the last thing I want to see and to have it happen when his wife is in a hospital bed after being missing for days is only making it worse.

"Laura has a concussion and bruises and minor cuts."

"So she might be disoriented or not remember everything that has happened."

"Yes, her doctor mentioned that," Elliott says.

I'm stuck watching Elliott and Joanna carefully. Their body language speaks volumes. After Elliott warned her away, he put distance between them. His arms are crossed, and he refuses to look her in the eye. No one around us would likely be able to put two-and-two together about their betrayal, but I know.

A nurse approaches, offering us a short, curt nod. "Mr. Bennett, we'll be able to let you in momentarily."

Elliott nods, his voice low. "Thank you."

Joanna shifts, glancing uneasily between Elliott and me

before she speaks again. "I'm going to grab a snack. Anyone want anything?"

Elliott shakes his head while I reply, "No, thank you."

She nods, retreating swiftly and disappearing around a corner.

Elliott turns to me and says, "I wonder how she knew to come here."

"She was talking to me at the coffee shop when you called. If it were up to me, she wouldn't be here."

"Why?"

I raise an eyebrow, taking a moment to breathe in deeply and manage the sudden spike of anger coursing through me. I debate whether or not I should say what is on the tip of my tongue, but I decide to keep things somewhat professional. "Laura's your wife. It's your responsibility to support her and not have any distractions. And I don't think I need to go any further than that."

"I'm not sure what you're talking about."

"Oh, I think you know exactly what I'm talking about."

He flinches at the sharpness in my tone. "Quinn, I... It's complicated."

"It always is," I reply, my voice laden with disdain.

A moment of silence ensues, but the tension is still there.

"Look," Elliott finally says, "we both want what's best for Laura, right? Let's keep the focus on her for now. Please."

I nod, my gaze drifting to the door behind him where Laura is. Getting into an argument about something I'm not directly involved in, especially when my friend is trying to recover from her trauma, isn't the best use of my time.

Just then, the door opens and a doctor steps out. "Family for Laura Bennett?"

"That's me," Elliott steps forward.

The doctor nods, beckoning him inside. Before he enters, Elliott casts a final look my way, eyes pleading for understanding.

"I'll be right here," I say as I settle into a nearby chair. I'm prepared to stay here for the long haul.

Hours pass by, and I find myself going crazy at Harrow Isle Hospital. Outside, the bitter cold of the evening is an odd complement to the sterile, controlled environment of the hospital. Its well-lit corridors make it easy to hear the echo of distant footsteps. The occasional beeping of machines and whispered conversations among patients and medical professionals become a monotonous noise in the background.

Each minute feels torturous. With each passing hour, my hope of seeing Laura or hearing any more news lessens. The plain, off-white walls of the waiting room seem to close in on me until I'm barely able to take any more of it.

When a nurse, her expression soft with empathy, approaches me, I brace myself. Her gentle suggestion that I head home and return in the morning is expected, but it still feels like a blow. The logical part of me knows she is right. I am mentally and physically drained. Yet leaving feels like abandoning Laura when she needs me most.

What I'm forced to remind myself is that Laura is in the best place she can be for what she is going through.

The hospital's vast parking lot is almost vacant as I slide into the driver's seat. I pick up my phone, its screen casting a soft glow in the dim interior of the car. I need to talk to someone. Anyone who might understand what I'm going through. I quickly type out a text to Elliott to let him know I was going back to the mansion and that I'll be back tomorrow.

There is only one person I can reach out to right now, but I still hesitate. He would want me to contact him about this, right? Throwing caution to the wind, my fingers begin flying across the screen.

> Me: Hey, are you working tonight?

The immediate appearance of the typing indicator is reassuring. I don't realize how much I am hoping for his reply until I see those three dots.

> Luke: Yes, but I have enough people here to cover for me. What's up?

> Me: I need to see you tonight. It's important.

I feel foolish typing this out, but it is the truth.

> Luke: Want to meet me at my house?

> Me: Yes.

I start the car and pull out of the parking spot, and in my mind, Luke's home is the light at the end of the tunnel. The streets look slightly familiar as I drive toward Luke's house. When I park my car in front of his home, he's already standing on his porch, waiting for me.

His embrace is everything I need. He doesn't ask any questions. He just holds me until the wind becomes too much and we move into the house. While we are in his cozy home, nothing else that comes from the outside world matters.

"I made some tea if you want some. And I have wine on

standby if you want that too."

I smile for the first time today. "While I would love a glass of wine, I think tea is a more suitable choice."

Once we are both settled on his couch, and I have a steaming mug of tea in my hand, I stare at the fireplace, trying to find the words that I want to say.

"I was at the hospital when I texted you," I say, just above a whisper. I can feel the weight of Luke's gaze on me, but I can't look at him right now.

"Wait, why?"

I take a deep breath and rip the figurative Band-Aid off. "It's Laura. She's been found, Luke." I turn my head so that my eyes meet his.

For a moment, he freezes. "Laura? Holy shit."

"I know." My voice quivers with a mix of relief and anxiety. "She was missing, and now she's in the hospital. She has a concussion, some bruises, minor cuts, but she's stable. It sounds like she's going to be okay."

Luke runs a hand through his hair, trying to process what I just said. "That's incredible. But also so shocking."

"Yeah, and we don't know exactly what happened. We don't know the full story yet." I sigh loudly as my index finger absentmindedly traces the rim of my cup. "She might be disoriented and might not remember certain things, but she's alive, Luke."

He leans closer to me. "And how are you holding up?"

"It's overwhelming," I confess as tears grow in the corner of my eyes. "One moment, I'm trying to figure out what happened to her, hoping that she's alive. Now she's back, and it's just a whirlwind of emotions. Relief, joy, confusion, all rolled up into one big ball."

Luke grabs my hand, covers it with his, and gives it a gentle squeeze. "I'm here for you. Whatever you need, I'm here."

"Thank you, Luke. It means the world to me."

We continue to talk and I'm grateful to have someone to share my thoughts and feelings about what I'm going through. It is almost as if he's the therapist and I'm the patient, a position I haven't been in in a long time. I appreciate him letting me vent while he just listens without passing judgment.

Just as I begin to feel something that resembles the calm and cool nature that I always try to embrace, my text notification sound shatters it completely. Once again, I'm on edge before Luke places his hand on my knee in an effort to calm me down again.

> Elliott: Thank you for coming here today and being there for Laura. I owe you more than I could ever pay back, but would you let me explain the things you alluded to this evening to Laura?

"What the—" I mumble, catching Luke's attention.

"What's wrong?" he asks, and I show him the message. I had already explained to him what I thought I knew about the situation in vague terms. But this is like a punch in the gut.

I don't know what to say and Luke mentions that I don't have to have an answer right now. This evening, filled with its highs and lows, has finally drawn to a close, and I need the reprieve.

22

QUINN

I open my eyes and take in my unfamiliar surroundings. For a second, I'm confused until I remember where I am, Luke's bed. As I sit up, I hear the sizzle of something cooking in the kitchen. The aroma of bacon and coffee is the next thing I notice, and my stomach lets me know that my body wants to be fed. I slip out of bed and walk out of the bedroom and into the short hallway.

From where I'm standing, I can see Luke at the stove with his back to me. When he shifts slightly, I can see him flipping pancakes while bacon crackles in a pan beside him. I love the picture this is painting, and I wish it could last forever.

But I don't belong in Harrow Isle permanently. And knowing that will keep me from exploring whatever is going on between us more.

"Morning," I say, leaning against the doorframe.

"Hey," Luke replies as he briefly looks over his shoulder. He sets another pancake onto a plate and reaches for the coffeepot. "Grab a seat. Breakfast is almost ready."

"Thank you."

I move to sit at his dining room table. The sunlight flickers through the trees outside and I love the way the light feels on my face. For a moment, I allow myself to forget about Laura, about the maddening unknowns surrounding her disappearance, and once Laura is on the mend, my departure from this island. I just want to be present, but I also know that it probably makes sense to talk about it today.

He sets a plate piled high with pancakes and bacon in front of me, then pours us both a mug of hot coffee. As I take my first bite, I'm struck by how perfectly fluffy the pancakes are, the crisp edges contrasting with the soft interior. The bacon is salty and crunchy, and the coffee is strong enough to clear the last remnants of sleep from my mind.

"Luke, this is amazing. Then again, I'm starting to wonder if there is anything you can't cook," I say between bites.

"Figured we could use a good meal to start the day," he replies, a hint of a smile playing at the corner of his mouth. "You look like you need it."

"If it were anyone else, I might take offense to that. But between you and me, I need this more than you know."

He chuckles softly, the sound echoing throughout the warm kitchen. "I've always prided myself on being a good judge of character, and right now, you're radiating *I need comfort food* vibes."

I smile, appreciating his lighthearted attempt to break the tension. After that, we quietly eat, savoring the food that is in front of us.

Before long, I can't take the silence anymore. Clearing my throat, I look into the depths of my coffee mug. "Luke, with Laura back. I've been thinking," I hesitate a bit, unsure of how to broach the subject.

He raises an eyebrow, curious. "About?"

"My time here on Harrow Isle," I say while looking anywhere but at him. "I came here for Laura. Now that she's home, I... I'm wondering if it's time for me to go back to Seattle. Now it won't be tomorrow, but once she's doing better, I'll have to head back home."

His fork clatters onto his plate. "I get it," he says slowly, and I can tell he's trying to choose his words carefully. "You want to return to your normal life."

I sigh and tuck my hair behind my ear. "I've been away from my home for so long now, but I also feel guilty about leaving."

Luke leans back in his chair. "Quinn, I understand that you're caught between two worlds right now. And I don't blame you for wanting to go back to something familiar. This has also been a traumatic experience for you."

"Thank you for understanding, but that's not it. Sure, Laura is a huge part of this, but you are a part of this too."

Luke looks genuinely taken aback. His gaze meets mine, and I can see the shock on his face. "Me? What do you mean?"

"It's just that you've become a constant for me here," I admit, my voice shaking slightly. "You've been supportive, understanding, and always there when I needed someone, including yesterday and today. And somewhere along the way, that bond became more important to me than I ever thought it would."

A heavy silence settles between us, charged with emotions I don't want to get into, and I assume that Luke feels the same.

"Quinn, I knew the chances of you leaving Harrow Isle

were high, but it didn't stop me from trying to get to know you. I was immediately drawn to you and no matter what you choose, I won't ever regret the time we've spent getting to know each other."

"Thank you," I say, and I swallow the emotions that threaten to unleash.

Luke stands up from the table and walks over to me, his gaze never leaving mine. I stand up too, and he wraps his strong arms around me in a warm embrace. I find myself melting into him because I feel safe and protected. The steady rhythm of his heartbeat against my ear is soothing, a quiet reassurance that he supports me no matter what.

"Thank you," I repeat as his chin comes to rest on the top of my head.

We stand like that for a moment, and I realize that I need this embrace too.

When my phone rings in my pocket, it forces me back into our reality. Reluctantly, I pull away, check to see who it is, and answer the call.

"Quinn, it's Elliott," he says as if I don't already know. "Laura wants to see you."

"Are you serious?"

"Absolutely, she specifically asked for you. I don't know why, but she did."

I glance up at Luke, who's watching me. "Alright, Elliott, I'll be there as soon as I can."

"Thank you. I know it means a lot to her and to me too," Elliott says before hanging up.

I can't shake the disbelief over Elliott's words, nor the anxiety over seeing Laura again after all this time, especially with what she is going through. I turn to Luke and say,

"Elliott said Laura wants to see me, but what about the hospital's family-only policy?"

"Maybe he found a way around it. I wouldn't be surprised if he called in a few favors to get this to happen."

Luke pauses, his eyes searching mine for a moment, gauging my reaction. "How do you feel about that? Seeing her, I mean."

I swallow the lump forming in my throat. "Nervous. Excited. Overwhelmed. A mix of everything, really."

"It's okay to feel all those things. And you don't have to rush. Take your time to process."

I nod slowly, trying to gather my thoughts. "It's just... how did she know to ask for me? She didn't know I was here for sure."

"Didn't you mention that she specifically asked for you to come if she disappeared? Maybe she knew that, without a doubt, you would come. Or Elliott could've told her you were here."

Either option is plausible, and I should have thought of both, but with everything going on, it feels like I can't think straight.

After a moment, I straighten up, determination settling within me. "Alright. I need to go see Laura. But first, a quick stop at the Bennett mansion to freshen up and change my clothes."

Luke nods, offering a supportive smile. "Call me when you're ready."

"I will," I say just before I place a kiss on his mouth.

Once I say goodbye to Luke, I head to my car, ready to see a friend that I hadn't seen in way too long.

23

QUINN

I take a deep breath as I push open the door to room 342. The walls, a dull, muted shade of blue, seem to absorb what little light filters through the partially drawn blinds. Cold linoleum stretches beneath my feet, and the steady, rhythmic beeping of Laura's heart monitor echoes through the small space.

Elliott sits in a chair near her bed, one hand in his lap, holding Laura's hand with the other. His face is pale as if the weight of the world is on his shoulders. How different he looks from the man who picked me up from the dock. He doesn't notice me in the room, I assume because he is lost in his own thoughts. But it's not him who needs my attention.

Laura lies motionless on the hospital bed, her once vibrant features now pale and gaunt. Tubes snake from her arms, disappearing into the tangle of medical equipment that surrounds her. The sight makes me feel terrible. But all these machines tell me that she is alive and that's the most important thing.

"Quinn, I didn't hear you come in."

I turn to find Elliott's gaze on me as he stands up. As far as I know, he's been here around the clock since Laura was found.

"Hey," is all I can muster because I'm unable to tear my gaze from Laura. My heart aches at the sight of her, but more importantly, she's alive.

But Allison probably isn't.

The thought shakes me to my core. I don't need to think about my little sister right now.

I watch as Laura's eyes flutter open, but she still looks disoriented. She scans the room until her gaze settles on me.

"Q—Quinn?" she says, her voice barely audible beneath the sounds of the beeping machines.

I swallow hard, forcing a shaky smile as I try to keep my emotions in check. I approach her bedside. "Hey, Laura. It's been a long time."

"Too long," she agrees with a ghost of a smile, her words slightly slurred. "I missed you."

"I missed you too." I pull up a chair and sit by her bedside.

Elliott's eyes find mine, and for a brief moment, a silent understanding passes between us. There's gratitude in his gaze but also a guarded caution. It's clear he's protective of Laura in her vulnerable state. Interesting how that has changed since Laura's voice memos.

"Remember that time," Laura begins, her voice stronger than before, "we snuck out to that abandoned house on the edge of campus? It was so creepy, but I insisted we explore it."

I chuckle softly as the memory appears in my head. If she wants to talk about the memories we have together, then I have no problem with it. "Of course I remember. I was terrified, but you didn't back down even though we could have gotten into a lot of trouble. You never let fear control you."

"Until now," she whispers, her gaze falling to the sterile sheets.

"Hey," I say, reaching out to touch her arm gently. "You're still here, Laura. You fought your way back to us. That's not someone who's given in to fear."

She tries to move, I assume, in an attempt to sit up. Her eyes meet mine, and I can see the frustration in them. I share a look with Elliott and together, we get up to help her.

"Thank you," she says to both of us.

"Of course," I say. "Anything you need, just let us know."

A comfortable silence passes between us until I open my mouth to speak. However, no words get out because a sudden commotion erupts outside the room. There are muffled voices, and the sound of footsteps outside our door.

There is a knock on the door and when it opens, my eyes widen in shock. Sheriff Murray walks into the room with a younger police officer.

"Elliott?" Sheriff Murray asks, his voice low and steady, with all the authority in the world. "We need to talk to you about Laura's disappearance."

If it weren't for the beeping of the machines that are hooked up to Laura, you could have heard a pin drop.

Elliott looks up at the two men who entered the room, his expression wavering between confusion and disbelief. His hands clench into fists and I'm not even sure he realizes he's done so. "I don't understand. I have nothing to do with putting her in this hospital bed."

"We just have a few questions and want you to come down to the station to answer them."

It's obvious to me that Sheriff Murray is trying to do this as quietly as possible and he's only asking nicely because he doesn't want to cause a scene. But I don't know if Elliott is going to go down without a fight.

"Absolutely not. I'm not leaving Laura," Elliott says with conviction.

"I would hate to have to put you in handcuffs. If you come with us, and we get this taken care of, you can get back to your wife sooner."

Elliott hesitates but then nods. He turns back to Laura and leans down to press a soft kiss on her forehead. "I'll be back soon."

He turns to me, and I nod, silently promising to take care of her while he is gone. Once the men leave the room, I look at Laura, who is already looking at me.

"Can you stay here until Elliott gets back?"

"Of course." I sit as my mind races with questions, each one more unsettling than the last. What could Elliott possibly have to do with Laura's disappearance? And why would the police be so insistent on questioning him now, just as she's been rescued?

"Would you like for Mrs. Fleming to pack some of your things and bring them here? I would do it, but I'm not going to leave your side until we know Elliott is okay."

"I don't understand how they could think he would do such a thing to me," she says with a sniffle.

"We don't have to talk about it right this second. You need your rest and I know it's hard not to be worried about Elliott, but you also need to focus on taking care of yourself and getting better."

I give her hand a small squeeze and return my gaze to

Laura. I find her watching me, a mixture of emotions dancing on her face.

The room, once filled with a reunion that veered slightly toward a happy one even in Laura's state, now is filled with our silence that weighs me down. But there's still the beeping of machines that have no issue reminding me of where I am and why Laura is in this bed.

"There's so much I need to tell you."

Laura's words bring me out of the daze I'm in and I put my full attention back on her. "We have plenty of time to talk about what happened. I don't want to stress you out. By the way, I have your phone in my purse."

She gives me a small nod, agreeing with my assessment. "Thank you."

As I grab her phone, Laura clears her throat and lets out a shaky breath. "I think it's time I tell you what happened to me."

My heart races, anticipation knotting my stomach. "Only if you're ready."

"I'm as ready as I'll ever be." She closes her eyes for a moment before she opens them back up. "I was in my office that evening, answering some emails, when I got a phone call from an unknown number. I—I knew it was from all the research I've been doing into Harrow Isle because the voice warned me about not digging into information I had no business knowing. That was when I created the voice memo that said if something happened to me, for the person to reach out to you. I heard a noise outside of my room and I waited a beat before reacting. Apparently that was a mistake because the next I knew everything went dark."

She takes a deep breath as she continues. "I woke up in a

cold room with my hands tied together with zip ties and tape put over my mouth. The days and nights that I was gone blurred together. I'm still not sure how long I was gone."

I want to tell her that this is something that she doesn't have to tell me. Reliving this must be painful and I can't imagine what she is going through.

"The person who kidnapped me, if I had to guess, was a tall, thin man. He's always masked and never speaks so I wasn't able to identify him. But he made a mistake. He left a paperclip nearby and it took some maneuvering for me to get it into the locking mechanism, but I failed. I couldn't open it. I tried rubbing up against the wall in the room to see if I could create some friction that might get me loose, but that failed too.

I glance down at her wrists and notice the bruising that indicates what Laura is telling me did happen.

"Finally, while he was gone, I must have worn the zip tie down enough because I was able to snap the tie open. I snuck out of the room I was in and found myself in an alley. Without a second thought, I ran for my life. I ran into a woman nearby who was eager to help me."

Tears blur my vision, and I blink them away. "Laura," I whisper, "you're incredible. You know that, right?"

She chuckles weakly. "I did what I needed to do to survive. And now I must rest. Talking took a lot out of me."

I'm not surprised. Laura closes her eyes and I watch as she rests. It still takes some time before I feel comfortable diverting my attention from her.

I manage to pull out my laptop and start to get to work, clearing out my inbox. After answering quite a few emails, I look up and notice that the sun is setting. Hours have passed without me realizing it. I glance over at Laura, who is still resting. A nurse came in a few minutes ago to check Laura's vitals, offering comforting smiles and words. But there isn't anything they can do to help relieve the stress coursing through this room.

However, I know of someone who might be able to help distract me temporarily. I pull out my phone and send a quick text message.

> Me: Laura is doing better than can be expected, but she's resting now. I'm the only one with her because Elliott has been taken in for questioning by Sheriff Murray.

It takes a few minutes for him to respond, but I'm grateful, nonetheless.

> Luke: Would my coming stress you out? I have some time before I need to be at the bar.

Considering the feud between their families, I'm surprised he offered to come. However, I'm also aware of how his presence will complicate matters. Before I can type, another message comes from him.

> Luke: I won't come near Laura's room. I just thought you might need someone to be there for you right now.

I reread his message several times before I am able to compose one of my own.

> Me: Would the hospital's cafeteria work?

Luke: Sounds good. See you soon.

I feel somewhat guilty about leaving Laura, but taking a ten-minute break to see Luke will recharge me.

I work on my computer once again until I get another text.

Luke: I'm in the cafeteria.

Glancing back at Laura, I whisper, "I'll be back soon." I doubt she hears me, but it makes me feel better.

With that, I leave Laura's room and head toward the hospital cafeteria, preparing myself to see Luke and, hopefully, find some clarity in this heavy fog of uncertainty.

24

QUINN

The familiar hum of soft conversations and the aroma of freshly brewed coffee greet me as I push open one of the doors to the hospital cafeteria. It's a welcome contrast to the constant beep of machines and the silence of Laura's room when she is resting,

The cafeteria isn't particularly crowded. It seems as if most of the tables are occupied by families of patients or by medical professionals who are snagging a quick break. I look around until I find him.

Luke is seated at a corner table, engrossed in his phone, and not paying attention to the world around him. Two cups of coffee sit in front of him, and I pray that they taste as good as the aroma makes me think they will.

When I'm within a couple of feet of his table, Luke looks up and his gaze lands on me. A smile appears on his face and it's just what I need right now.

"Hey," he says softly, pushing one of the coffee cups toward the empty spot across from him.

"Hey," I repeat, sliding into the chair. The warmth of the

mug seeps through my fingers, comforting me. "Thanks for the coffee."

He nods. "Of course. Thought you could use it. How's Laura?"

Taking a sip, I let Luke's question hang in the air while I distract myself with the coffee. It is an excellent decision. "She's stable and I was able to talk to her. But the stuff with Elliott... my mind is still completely blown by it."

Luke lets out a long breath. "Yeah. And just before I came here, I heard one of our regulars talking to one of Harbor's Edge bartenders about how Elliott is experiencing financial troubles."

That makes me do a double take and I'm grateful I wasn't drinking that coffee when he said it. "Seriously?"

Luke nods. "Now, I can't confirm anything, but apparently, it's churning through the gossip mill."

"Wow, I didn't get much of an impression of that outside of the crumbling state of their home, but I thought that might have been on purpose." I pause for a second, thinking about this new information. "Could this all be connected? Does Sheriff Murray think that Elliott is involved now due to new information?"

Luke shrugs. "It could be, and you still don't have all of the pieces yet."

I don't want to jump to conclusions, but I need to say the following statement. "Could Elliott have hired someone to kidnap his wife to get..."

Luke leans in closer to me and says, "It doesn't really make sense, right? There was no ransom and if there was, it would have been Elliott paying it versus being paid it."

"Yeah, I agree," I say as I see a flicker of movement behind him, distracting me. I glance over his shoulder, and my heart lurches painfully in my chest.

Standing near the entrance of the cafeteria is a girl who is around the age of eight. Her hair is a shade I recognize all too well, and her eyes, also, because they mirror mine. She's watching me with a vacant look.

"Allison?" I whisper, not believing what appears in my vision.

Luke, following my gaze, turns around. By the time he turns back to me, his expression is pure confusion. "Who's Allison?"

I don't answer him immediately, my attention is still locked on the girl. But as quickly as she appears, she vanishes. My heart is pounding, but I can't make myself get up to see if I can get closer to her.

"Quinn? Quinn!" Luke's voice breaks through my trance. "Hey, are you okay?"

Allison, my little sister, was kidnapped when she was eight years old during my freshman year. And we never found out what happened to her. I wasn't able to be there for her because I was away at college. Laura had been there for me when everything happened, and I would forever be grateful for her.

"I—I thought I saw her, Luke. My sister. Allison." My hands are shaking uncontrollably.

Luke's hand covers mine. "Would it help you to talk about it?"

For a moment, I hesitate. The pain of Allison's disappearance is something I thought I had done a good job of locking away. But with everything going on, clearly, I've failed.

"She was the sweetest person," I start, not trusting my

voice to stay strong. "Always laughing, always curious. Although I haven't heard it in so long, her laughter is something I won't ever forget."

Luke listens to me without interrupting and only nods occasionally. The cafeteria, once bustling with noise, seems to fade into the background.

"The day she disappeared." I swallow hard, feeling the weight of the years I've spent wondering, hoping, and mourning. "It was just a normal day. My mom said she was playing outside, and she turned my back for one second and then she was gone."

"Saying I'm sorry doesn't seem to be enough."

I sigh. "I get that, and I've heard it a lot. It's something I've learned to live with, but every so often, like today, something triggers it, and it feels like everything happened yesterday."

We sit in silence for a moment before Luke finally speaks. "It's understandable why you'd think you saw her, especially after everything that's happened recently."

I nod, grateful for his understanding. "It's just... hard. And seeing that girl, it felt so real."

Luke gives my hand another squeeze. "We'll get to the bottom of Laura's situation. And who knows, maybe along the way, you'll find some peace when it comes to Allison."

I nod slowly. "Maybe."

25

QUINN

A Few Days Later

I watch as Elliott gently adjusts the cushions behind Laura's back as she sits down on the couch. Her blonde hair cascades down one side, Elliott insisting on brushing it for her and making sure that every strand is perfectly in place. He's even made sure that most things are in within arm's reach for her in case she needs to grab things when either Elliott, Mrs. Fleming, Mr. Gregory, or I are busy. I think it is a little bit of overkill now that Laura is able to stand and walk on her own, albeit a little slowly, but it is sweet that he's taking care of her. Plus, our shared concern for her has brought us together in unexpected ways. We are happy that she is finally home and is recovering nicely, according to the doctors caring for her.

"Could you hand me that blanket, Quinn?" Elliott asks.

I nod, reaching for the soft throw draped over the armchair. I pass it to him and take a step back.

"Thank you." Elliott spreads the blanket over Laura's legs with care.

"Can I have a glass of water, please?" Laura asks.

Without missing a beat, Elliott makes a move to get it for her first. He pours a glass from the crystal-clear pitcher on the side table and hands it to her. She's getting better each day, and I'm convinced it is in strong part to Elliott taking care of her every need since Sheriff Murray allowed him to come back home. She really doesn't have to lift a finger.

"Quinn," Laura says after swallowing a sip of water. She runs a hand through her hair before she speaks again. "Thank you for everything, including being here for me."

"Always," I reply, the word heavy with memories of our college days when it felt as if the world was ours. Neither one of us speaks and I can see in her eyes that she feels the same.

"We're grateful for you dropping everything and coming to help find Laura," Elliott adds.

"Thank you, Elliott." His words are unexpected but appreciated.

This is the most relaxed I've been since I got here, and I am grateful for it. It means that all of this is coming to an end. Just when I decide that I am going to give Elliott and Laura some time alone, there is a loud knock at the door. My heart leaps into my throat, and I exchange a wary glance with Elliott and then Laura.

"Stay here," Elliott says as he moves toward the entrance.

I nod and peek into the foyer just as Elliott is about to open the door.

When Elliott swings the door open, I see Sheriff Murray flanked by two officers, their faces grim.

"Good afternoon, Sheriff," Elliott says. "How can I help you?"

"Apologies for the intrusion," he replies, his gaze sweeping the room before settling on Laura. "We've had a break in the case. We thought it best to inform you all in person."

My stomach drops to my feet. What have they discovered?

"Please," Elliott says, stepping aside to allow them entry. "Come in."

As they cross the threshold, I brace myself for what they are going to say.

Sheriff Murray's gaze locks onto mine, and I feel a cold shiver creep up my spine. "We have reason to believe we've found the person responsible for Laura's kidnapping."

"Who?" Elliott demands.

"Malcolm Gregory," Sheriff Murray says but doesn't elaborate further.

I can't process the news that I've just been given. The man who had been so quiet and mostly kept to himself from what I could see had kidnapped Laura?

"Are you sure?" Laura whispers from the couch, her voice trembling.

"Quite sure, ma'am." Sheriff Murray glances at the officers flanking him. "We've gathered enough evidence, to make an arrest. Security footage has been made available, and we found his fingerprints at where Laura was being held. Not to mention the anonymous tip we received."

As if on cue, two additional officers haul Mr. Gregory into the room. His hands are cuffed behind him, his face pale and drawn. He casts a wild-eyed glance at each of us before settling on Laura, his expression unreadable.

"Please, Mrs. Bennett," he says, desperation lacing his voice. "Tell them they've got it all wrong."

My heart pounds in my chest as I take in the scene before me. I'm still trying to process what is going on, let alone seeing Mr. Gregory in handcuffs.

"Take him away," Sheriff Murray orders.

The officers comply, maneuvering Mr. Gregory out of the room and onto the doorstep. I move toward the door, and I watch as they load him into the waiting squad car.

Out of the corner of my eye, I see movement and I turn slightly to see Mrs. Fleming standing in the doorway leading toward the dining room. After her conversation with Mr. Gregory the other day, I can't help but wonder if she was the one who called in the anonymous tip. But who turned the security footage over?

"Is it over?" Laura asks. "Can we finally start to put all this behind us?"

Sheriff Murray hesitates before answering. "Hopefully," he says softly. "But there's still work to be done. We're going to make sure that this is ironclad, Mrs. Bennett. We'll be in touch if anything else comes up." With that, the two officers that came to Elliott and Laura's door depart, leaving us standing in the suddenly silent living room.

I glance at Laura, her chest rising and falling in shallow breaths. Elliott hurries to be with her and as he sits down next to her, she leans against him.

"Sheriff Murray," I say, turning to face him once more as he lingers by the door. "There's one thing I don't understand. Why was Elliott considered a suspect?"

The sheriff shifts uncomfortably. "We had our reasons, but mostly we wanted to talk to him to confirm a few things. Now that Malcolm is in custody, our focus has shifted to uncovering the full extent of his involvement and if he's done this to anyone else on the island."

I think about the other disappearances I found when researching in the library. Based on how old I think he is, it's possible he could have been involved with those crimes as well.

Laura looks around the room and then she meets my gaze, her voice barely above a whisper. "Will we be safe now?"

Something about the way she says it tugs at the back of my mind. There's a subtle undertone, something not quite right. I try to reassure her, but by now, doubts are creeping in. "I hope so. Especially if the police believe they have the right person."

She nods slowly, her gaze drifting away. I can't shake the feeling though. Why would Laura doubt our safety now, after they've arrested Mr. Gregory? Is there something more she's not telling me?

"Mr. Gregory will be behind bars for a long time," Sheriff Murray adds his opinion as a way to reassure her. "You can rest easy knowing that justice will be served."

I escort Sheriff Murray to the door, and once I close it behind him, I turn to face Laura and Elliott. We exchange glances, and I, for one, am wondering where we go from here. For the first time in what feels like an eternity, we can finally breathe.

Laura's grip on Elliott tightens as they share a knowing

look. The nightmare is over, but picking up the pieces has just begun.

I walk toward the couple and say, "I think with this wrapping up, it's time for me to be heading home. I'll pack my things, and then, hopefully, we can schedule a boat to pick me up in two days?"

"I can arrange that. Thank you," Elliott says quietly. "For everything. I don't know how we would have made it through all of this without your help."

I give them a small smile, grateful that they're finally safe and sound again. "I'm glad I was able to help even though I didn't do much. You saved yourself and I'm so grateful that you did. Let's make plans to meet up again soon under happier circumstances."

Laura moves to tuck a piece of her blonde hair behind her ear and gives me the first big smile I've seen from her. "I'd love that. I really would."

26

QUINN

The morning sun, a soft golden orb, peeks over the horizon, casting its warm glow upon the tranquil island. Birds serenade the dawn with their melodic songs, and it feels like a brand-new century. This feels like a rebirth of sorts, and it makes me feel sad about my departure from this island.

As I stand on the porch taking in the serene scene before me, I see Laura approaching out of the corner of my eye. I'm happy to see her up and about again. Our gazes meet as she takes another step forward, slowly opening her arms wide, and I accept the invitation, stepping in for a light hug.

"I know it's all that I've been saying, but I can't begin to thank you enough for everything you've done."

"Hey," I pull back slightly and look into her eyes. "That's what friends are for, right?"

"What you did was above and beyond what many friends would do."

"I don't think so. People care about each other. Plus, you came home with me and were there for me when Allison went missing. I couldn't afford to lose you too." There. My admission of the fear I had about losing Laura is finally out in the open and it feels good to get it off my chest.

Laura nods as tears appear in her eyes, her gaze not leaving mine. I glance over at Elliott, who has been standing off to the side, watching our exchange. He steps forward, and before I can react, he wraps me in an unexpected hug.

"Thank you, Quinn," he murmurs into my hair, his voice heavy with emotion. "For everything."

I hesitantly return the hug, not exactly sure how to react.

"Take care of her, Elliott," I say softly, and I stare at him for a moment longer than necessary. I'm alluding to him finally coming clean about his affair with Joanna, and when he gives me a small nod, I know that he has gotten the message.

"I will," he promises, his gaze steady and sincere.

The sound of gravel under tires draws our attention away from one another, and I see Luke coming down the driveway.

Once Luke parks his car, he approaches with measured steps. He nods toward Elliott. "Morning."

Elliott responds with a curt nod, his face betraying no emotion. "Luke."

Before anyone can say anything else, Luke extends his hand toward Elliott. It is a bold move, one that clearly takes Elliott by surprise. There is a pause, the air thick with anticipation as Laura and I look on. Then, after what feels like an eternity, Elliott takes it. Their handshake is brief but significant.

"I hope you both have a lovely time together," Laura comments, her tone cheerful, but I can sense an underlying caution in her words.

"Thanks," I say as Luke grabs my bags. "I'll see you all again soon."

Luke and I head to his car. With one last glance back at the Bennetts, I climb into Luke's vehicle. As we begin to pull away, I can see Laura whispering something to Elliott, a concerned look on her face, before she turns and gives us a wave.

"Quite the view, isn't it?" Luke says softly as we drive away from the Bennett estate, my gaze on the sideview mirror. I turn to stare at the window as I take in the scenery around me. It feels as if the weight of the world has been lifted, and now the sun is out. This area still seems creepy to me, but at least the sun is shining.

"It is. It feels as if a cloud has been lifted."

"Are you ready for tomorrow?" he asks, his voice gentle, but I can hear the hesitancy in his tone.

I swallow hard, my throat tight with anxiety. "I am, but I feel a mixture of emotions about it," I admit. "But I have to go home."

Luke nods solemnly, seemingly lost in his own thoughts as well. I'm sure he's also thinking about my departure tomorrow. It's all I can think about. That, and how much I really don't want to leave him behind.

We continue driving, winding through the narrow roads of Harrow Isle. The dense woods, the occasional glimpse of the sea shimmering under the sunlight, and the quaint houses that occasionally dot the landscape, everything seems brighter today, more vivid.

After a moment, Luke breaks the silence. "You know, Harrow Isle has a way of making you feel like you're in a different world. A place where time slows down. You came here to help your friend and, I believe, to find answers for yourself. I hope you found some. But the island, it's going to miss you."

I chuckle softly. "That's a weird thing to say. Can an island miss someone?"

He smiles. "Maybe not the land itself. But the people on it surely can. And some more than others." He glances at me, and for a brief moment, our eyes lock. It takes everything in me not to giggle at what he's trying to hint at.

I take a deep breath. "Luke, I'm going to miss you. A lot."

I watch as his grip tightens on the steering wheel. "I'll miss you too, Quinn. A lot more than I thought I would when we first met."

"I'll take that as a win."

I smirk when Luke chuckles under his breath. The car takes a turn, revealing a breathtaking view of the cliffs over-looking the ocean. He parks the car by the side, and we get out, both of us drawn to the mesmerizing view. The roaring waves crashing against the cliffs seem to echo the emotions inside of me.

We stand there, side by side. The wind in my hair feels magical, and I wish this would have been why I came here instead of being here to rescue my friend. The silence between us speaks volumes, but it's not uncomfortable.

Finally, Luke speaks, "You know, if you ever feel the need to come back, even if it's just to visit, you'll always have a place here."

"That's very sweet. I appreciate it."

Luke pulls me into a big hug, and after spending several minutes like that, we get back in Luke's car and drive around Harrow Isle, finding other places to visit and explore.

When the sun starts to set, Luke makes a turn onto a familiar road. "I figured it was time to head back to my place."

I smile, nodding. "Sounds perfect."

We pull up to Luke's cozy cottage, surrounded by tall trees and wilderness. The setting sun casts a golden hue over everything, and the scene looks like something out of a book.

We bring my things into his home, but we don't stop there. We continue to the back of the house and his backyard, which takes my breath away. A spacious lawn with beautifully manicured edges and a firepit surrounded by comfortable chairs.

Luke lights up the firepit, and the soft glow illuminates the space, creating a beautiful ambience. We settle down on the chairs and wrap ourselves in blankets to ward off the evening chill.

As the sun gets lower in the sky, we debate what we're going to eat for dinner. Once we eat, we settle in our chairs and Luke hands me a beer.

"This is incredible," I say as I stare up at the sky, lost in the vastness of the universe above.

"I love sitting out here. I don't do it as often as I should."

The evening stretches on, and we share a blend of deep conversations and moments that lighten the mood. My looming departure casts a bittersweet shadow over us, but for now, in this very moment, everything feels just right.

THE NEXT MORNING, I find myself staring at the water before us. Luke has driven me to the marina and now it is time to say goodbye. Luke leans in and our lips meet in a tender kiss that speaks volumes about the bond we've formed. The hold he has on my face anchors me to him, and I wish that I didn't have to let go. When we pull away, I look into his eyes, and he speaks first.

"Take care, Quinn," he whispers.

"You too, Luke," I reply as my fingers brush against the stubble on his cheek.

With one last look, I step onto the boat, feeling the weight of the distance already growing between us. My boatman places my bags on the boat and soon the engine roars to life.

Before the boat can pull away, I watch as Luke checks his phone and puts it to his ear. Immediately, the expression on his face changes. Before I know it, I see Luke waving frantically, trying to get my attention. I jump up and tell the boatman, and he's able to turn the engine off. By that time, Luke runs down the dock toward us, and his face is completely drained of color.

"Quinn!" he yells out, his voice strained. "It's Elliott... He's dead."

27

QUINN

My brain can't compute what is going on. All I can do is replay the scene of Luke getting the fateful phone call just before I was to set sail for home.

There is no way this is happening.

None of this is true.

The conversation between Luke and I is almost nonexistent. There is really nothing to say.

Elliott Bennett is dead.

Once we hit the gravel at the Bennett estate, it is clear that this, in fact, is real. Police vehicles are parked all over the place, and I can't help but wonder if they will even let us get close to the house.

But I have to try to be there for Laura.

Once Luke finds a place to park, we step out of the car, but the only people we see outside of the home are police officers. As we make our way to the double doors, Sheriff Murray looks over at us and waves us in, allowing us to bypass the police officer who is standing watch near the door.

The moment Luke and I cross the threshold, all we hear are the sounds of cries and the voices of people trying to offer condolences. The home has transcended into even more darkness with the echoes of sorrow that now seem to be bouncing off the walls.

I feel Luke's hand on my back as if he's guiding me through all of this, and I'll take his strength right now, especially since Laura is going to need me to support her.

I walk into the living room and find Laura, who is surrounded by Joanna and Mrs. Fleming. It's obvious to me that Joanna is barely holding on, and I know that she is crying for a multitude of reasons, including losing her lover.

But my focus quickly turns back to Laura. Her hair is in disarray, her eyes are red-rimmed from crying, and her hands tremble as she clutches a tissue. When she looks up and spots me, I see the visible signs of relief flowing through her body.

"Quinn," Laura whispers. She meets my gaze, and for a fleeting moment, we share an unspoken understanding of the pain tearing through us both, although I'd been living through my pain for longer.

"Hey," I say softly, crossing the room to join their huddled group. "I'm so sorry, Laura."

"I—I can't believe he's gone," Laura manages to say.

"None of us can." Joanna lays a comforting hand on Laura's shoulder, despite fighting back tears of her own.

"Everything feels like a nightmare. And I keep waiting to wake up, but I never do."

I reach out and take Laura's hand, giving it a gentle squeeze. "You're not alone in this. We are all here to help you manage this."

"Thank you," Laura says again, her voice quivering. "It means so much to know I have people who care."

A flash of Laura's voice memo appears in my mind, with her talking about the attention and care that Elliott gave her. But I push it to the side.

As Laura's sobs continue to rack her body, I glance around at Joanna and Mrs. Fleming, both of their eyes brimming with tears. I take a deep breath and speak the words I hope will offer some semblance of comfort.

"I'm so sorry, Laura." The therapist in me wants to dig deep and find the words to say that might provide some relief, but I don't have many. "Laura, we are all here for you to lean on. We will help you navigate this."

"Ms. Pierce is right," Mrs. Fleming adds, taking my cue. "We're all here for you, Laura."

As we sit together, I become aware of someone staring at me. I turn to look and find Luke staring at me, but he's standing off to the side.

"Luke," I acknowledge, giving him a small, sad smile. He simply responds with a subtle nod, and I'm thankful to have him here with me.

"I just don't understand why..." Laura says, sniffling. "Why Elliott? After everything we've been through, why?"

Her words are barely coherent, but I'm able to put together what she's saying.

"Sometimes, things don't make sense right away, especially when it's completely senseless," I admit. "But eventually, we'll find answers."

Joanna shares a look with me as she continues to console Laura. I look around and briefly take in the quiet voices of the police and medical professionals who are trying to do their jobs.

"I wish we had more information," Mrs. Fleming mumbles and I'm not sure if she meant to say it out loud or not.

Laura snaps her head and looks at her with a heated glare. "He was just sitting in his chair! He wasn't in bed when I woke up this morning, and I went to check on him and he was just fucking there. Not moving, not breathing." She takes in a huge gulp of air, and I'm left wondering if she might pass out. I shift my body so that if she does, I can be there to hopefully take the brunt of the fall.

"I heard someone say it could be a heart attack, but they wouldn't be sure until he has an autopsy. It makes no sense though because he took care of himself!"

The room falls silent at her outburst. Everyone allows her to vent, and no one corrects the assumption that people who are physically fit don't have heart attacks. It is important for her to get her thoughts and feelings out.

Laura's face is pale again, but thankfully she sits down again. "He was fine last night; how could he be dead in the morning?" she begins whispering to herself repeatedly. Her voice grows hoarser with each word she utters.

Suddenly, Joanna jumps up and pulls her phone out of her pocket. She glances down at the screen and looks back up at Laura, looking frazzled. "Is it okay if I take this call?"

Laura just nods her head, and I watch Joanna leave the room.

Everyone turns as someone nearby clears their throat and we find Sheriff Murray standing just off to the left of us. He walks around and comes to stand near Laura before pulling one of the armchairs over so that he can sit right in front of her.

"Laura, first, I want to say how terribly sorry I am that all of this has happened. Elliott was a pillar of the community, and we'll miss him deeply."

"Thank you," Laura murmurs as she looks down at her hands.

"I hate that I have to ask you this, but we want to get this information while it's still fresh in your head. Can you walk me through the last time you saw him alive?"

Laura tucks a piece of her hair behind her ear and sighs. It's as if she's trying to gather the strength to talk and I don't blame her one bit. "I last saw him last night. He made sure that I had everything I needed before I went to bed. He told me that he was going to stay up a couple more hours and then he'd join me."

"Do you know if he came to bed last night?"

Laura shook her head. "I don't think he did. His side of the bed was still made when I woke up. And that was why I went downstairs. To see where he was and... and..."

A fresh set of sobs begins, and Sheriff Murray reaches forward and grabs Laura's hand, his way of apologizing, I assume. "Given the sudden nature of Elliott's death, we're recommending an autopsy. It's standard in cases like these to ensure there's no foul play and to provide clarity on the cause of death."

Laura looks up at him. "An autopsy? But I thought they were saying he just had a heart attack."

Sheriff Murray tries to comfort her. "That's what it seems like as of now, but an autopsy will confirm it. If there are any suspicions, a toxicology report will also be ordered as part of the process. It's just a step to ensure full transparency and get the answers we want."

I bite back the sigh that threatens to leave my lips. The situation, the suddenness of it all, is overwhelming for me, let alone Laura. I can only imagine the storm of emotions Laura is experiencing. The thought of your spouse dying and then you discovering their body is... indescribable.

I stand up and say, "I'm going to stretch my legs a bit. Does anyone need anything?"

The group shakes their heads, and as I walk past Luke, I reach my hand out to touch his and continue walking toward the back of the house.

As I near one of the many doors in this house, I pause. Although it is muffled by the wooden barrier, I can hear Joanna's voice and I realize I stumbled onto her having her phone call. "All I meant to do was scare him a little and get him to start thinking about our exit strategy. And if people find out about us... about the money I owe him..."

My mouth drops open as I press my ear closer to make sure that I'm catching all of this.

"We had plans. We were going to sort it all out. Now what am I going to do?" There's a sniffle. "If this comes out, if people know we were sleeping together and about the money..."

There's a momentary silence before I hear her whisper, "He was going to help me. It was supposed to be our secret."

With every word she says, the weight in my chest grows heavier. Joanna and Elliott were involved, and not just romantically. The depth of their entanglement, the money, the lies, the secrecy—it paints a complex picture. And, I assume, all of this was kept from Laura.

She lets out a harsh breath. "I shouldn't be talking about this here."

I step away from the door, taking it as my cue to leave, as she will likely be exiting the room soon. I decide to keep what I've just learned to myself for now. Laura should know about this, but I need to figure out a way to tell her.

28

QUINN

I watch through the window as Joanna's car pulls into the driveway. Her face is still pale, much like it was yesterday. I make a move toward the door after I watch her exit the vehicle.

"Joanna," I call out as she walks up the front steps. "Thanks for coming."

"Of course," she replies, her eyes darting around nervously. "I want to be there for Laura as much as I can be."

"I know she appreciates it." I force a smile, but it's definitely fake. I move so that Joanna can step past me and enter the Bennett mansion's foyer.

"Laura is in the living room," I inform Joanna and motion for her to follow me.

She nods, her fingers twisting the strap of her purse as we walk across the room and toward the living room. Nervous energy is jumping off her in spades and I wonder if it has to do with the call I overheard her having yesterday.

"Quinn," she whispers, stopping me just outside the living

room door. "There's something I need to tell you. But not here—not now. Can we talk later?"

"Sure," I say, trying not to appear concerned. "We'll find some time alone."

"Thank you." She gives me a small, grateful smile before stepping into the room where Laura is waiting for the both of us.

As Joanna and I sit down on either side of Laura as she talks to the funeral director, I can't help but watch Joanna. Her eyes dart around the room as if searching for an escape while her hands tremble ever so slightly as she clutches her purse. The lines etched on her forehead and the tightness in her jaw also betray her nervousness, although she attempts to show that she is calm.

I turn away from Joanna temporarily and pay more attention to Laura. As the funeral director is asking her questions, Laura appears almost detached, her face a blank canvas, void of emotion. I'm not surprised, given the amount of trauma that she's gone through the last several days and what she is continuing to deal with. I don't think she will be able to start the process of healing until Elliott is buried and all this attention shifts behind her. Even when she begins to heal, things will never be the same for her ever again.

There's a knock on the door that forces our focus to who is standing on the other side. Mrs. Fleming moves to open the door and we watch Sheriff Murray and a woman step into the foyer.

"Sorry to interrupt," Sheriff Murray says, stepping into the room with a manila envelope clutched in his hand. His voice is heavy, weighed down with the burden of the news he's about to deliver. "This is Dr. Samson, and we have the preliminary autopsy results on Elliott."

Laura turns and looks at the funeral director and says, "If you'll excuse us for a moment."

The funeral director gathers his things and makes his way out of the room while Sheriff Murray and Dr. Samson make their way in.

Every second they don't say a word makes my stomach drop further.

"Let's hear it," Laura speaks up, finally showing signs of emotion. Her jaw is set, her knuckles white as she clenches her hands together. "I want Quinn and Joanna to be here to listen to this with me."

It is as if she wants to get it done as quickly as possible, and I don't blame her one bit.

Dr. Samson clears her throat before beginning. "Firstly, my deepest condolences for your loss. This is always a difficult part of my job." There's genuine sorrow in her eyes. "Upon our preliminary examination, there are a few irregularities in Mr. Bennett's condition."

"What do you mean, irregularities?" Laura's voice quivers slightly, but her gaze remains sharp.

Dr. Samson continues, "The initial findings don't align perfectly with a natural heart attack. It's possible, yes, but something seems off."

Laura's voice is barely above a whisper, "Are you saying there might be another reason for Elliott's death?"

Dr. Samson hesitates, choosing her words carefully. "We can't confirm that as of now, but it's one of the possibilities we're considering. A detailed toxicology report is in the process. It will give us a clearer picture of what happened."

Joanna's eyes narrow slightly. "Do you think someone might have killed Elliott?"

I can't help but remember the overheard conversation and Joanna's desperate financial situation. I cast a glance at her, but she avoids my gaze.

Sheriff Murray speaks up this time. "It's standard procedure to consider all angles. We'll continue our investigation and see what we find."

"Thank you for letting us know," I say because I think everyone else in the room is shell-shocked and doesn't know how to process the news.

The room becomes silent as Dr. Samson leaves, and we all digest the news. I can't pinpoint the emotions that are coursing through me, let alone start trying to figure out what everyone else in the room is feeling.

Laura's soft whisper breaks the silence. "This can't be happening."

Her eyes are raw from the countless tears she's cried, and they dart around the room as though looking for an escape, a way to get out of here after the latest news we were told. Her fingers tremble as she tries to compose herself. It's now evident that disbelief is at the forefront of her mind, probably sitting right next to shock.

My attention involuntarily drifts to Joanna. She's shifted back into being more nervous than anything, clearly uncomfortable with what we'd just been told. She avoids eye contact, her gaze distant and unfocused. The memory of that phone call she took and the urgency in her voice replay in my mind as I begin to wonder if she played a role in all of this.

Sheriff Murray clears his throat, trying to bring our attention back to him. "I need to know where everyone was the night before Elliott died. Any detail you will be able to provide might be relevant," he states.

"Can I first walk the funeral director to the door, and then we can conduct all of the interviews you want?"

Sheriff Murray nods and Laura slowly gets up. I watch from a distance as she quietly talks to the funeral director and escorts him out the door. Then she turns to Mrs. Fleming, who joins us in the living room.

"We are ready to do whatever you need us to do. I can also call in the rest of the staff here to have them give statements," Laura says. It's the most stoic I've seen her, and this might be for the best at the moment.

Sheriff Murray looks around the room, his eyes pausing for a moment longer on each of our faces. "That works for me. Given the sensitive nature of the matter, I'd like to take your statements individually," he finally says. "Joanna, if you don't mind, we'll start with you."

Laura motions toward another office across the hallway. "You can use that room, Sheriff. It'll give you the privacy you need."

Joanna hesitates, then exhales loudly. She rises from her seat, straightening her blouse and avoiding everyone's gaze as she follows Sheriff Murray into the study, closing the door behind her.

I can't help but steal a glance at Laura, whose face remains unreadable. Mrs. Fleming looks out of place here and potentially sick to her stomach. The distant murmurs of the conversation between Joanna and Sheriff Murray make it impossible to understand what Joanna is saying or what questions the sheriff is asking her. Her stay in the room seems long, but I don't have anything to judge it on. By the time she emerges, her face is a shade paler, and she avoids meeting anyone's eyes.

Mrs. Fleming is next, her steps reluctant. Her statement is shorter than Joanna's, and when she returns, she looks visibly shaken.

Laura offers, "Would you like to go to your room, Mrs. Fleming?"

She nods, whispering her thanks, and leaves the living room.

Now it's Laura's turn. She takes a deep breath before she stands up to walk into the study. She gives me a short glance and heads toward the office. I wait until the door clicks shut behind her to look away.

There is about a minute or two of silence before Joanna breaks it. "I can't believe that we are living in this nightmare."

I look up at her as I rub my temples. "None of us can, Joanna. This is absolutely unbelievable."

I notice a flash of vulnerability in her eyes before she responds. "Quinn, there are things you don't know. Some factors at play here."

I narrow my eyes because I'm over this sidestepping around the truth. "What things? Do they have anything to do with the affair you were having with Elliott?"

Joanna's face becomes noticeably red. "How did you...?"

I raise an eyebrow, unwilling to let her deflect. "That question doesn't matter. Is it true?"

She exhales shakily, her eyes landing on her lap. "Yes, it's true. W—we started a few months ago. It was never meant to be serious. But it just... happened."

I debate with myself about whether it's worth pointing

out that *it just happened* isn't really a thing, but I refrain. Instead, I ask, "Did Laura know?"

Joanna bites her lip, obviously struggling. "I'm not completely sure. She never said anything to me, and as far as I know, never said a word to Elliott. I told Sheriff Murray because the likelihood of it coming out during his investigation is high."

I can't help but wonder if she also told him about the money Elliott lent her, but it wasn't a question I should ask. "When are you going to tell Laura? She deserves to know."

"Probably after the funeral. I don't want to cause her any more stress right now. It would also help me come to terms with what I assume will be the end of our friendship."

It takes everything within me to stop myself from rolling my eyes. Now I wish I could bring Elliott back from the dead so that he could give his wife the truth she deserves to have.

Joanna's eyes shimmer with tears. "I never wanted any of this. I wish I could turn back time."

"Don't we all?" I murmur, staring into the distance until a noise forces me to turn my head.

Laura walks out of the office and her gaze turns to mine. "It's your turn, Quinn."

29

QUINN

The crimson glow of the digital recorder is taunting me, daring me to say the wrong thing. It takes some effort, but I shift my gaze to Sheriff Murray, who sits opposite me in one of the offices in the Bennett mansion. I'm trying to ignore the knot tightening in my stomach as I prepare to start this interview.

"Quinn," Sheriff Murray begins, looking down at the notepad he put next to the recorder. His gravelly voice cuts through my thoughts. "Can you please recount your whereabouts the evening of Elliott Bennett's death?"

I swallow hard, forcing myself to meet his unwavering gaze. "I was with Luke Hartley most of that day and all of the evening. He picked me up from here that morning and then we spent the day and evening together before he took me to the marina to go head back to Seattle the following morning."

"And Luke will confirm this?" Sheriff Murray presses, leaning back in his chair.

"Yes, he will," I say firmly, meeting his gaze head-on.

Inside, my heart is thundering against my rib cage, but I refuse to let my fear show. It might indicate to Sheriff Murray that I'm not being truthful when I am.

Sheriff Murray makes a note in his pad and looks up at me again. "Did you, at any point that evening, speak to Elliott Bennett, whether in person, on the phone, or through any other means?"

"No," I reply, shaking my head. "I hadn't seen Elliott since the morning I left. He thanked me for all that I'd done with trying to help find Laura, and that was it."

He jots down another note. "Has Elliott ever mentioned any concerns or fears to you? Perhaps something related to personal or business matters? Anything unusual in the days leading up to his death?"

I hesitate, searching my memories to see if I can recall anything. "Elliott didn't share any concerns with me outside of being worried about Laura because of her disappearance. We weren't that close. In fact, before Laura disappeared, I'd only met him a handful of times, but that was because of my friendship with Laura."

Sheriff Murray nods. "Any idea why anyone might want to harm him? Given the recent findings, we are not ruling out any possibilities."

Again, I take a moment before answering, "Elliott was a prominent figure in the community, and I've heard through some town gossip that the Bennetts weren't all that well liked for the most part. I don't know enough to speculate, however."

"Is there anything else you think might be relevant to our investigation?"

"Yes, I overheard a conversation between Elliott and

Joanna that might be of interest too." I proceed to tell him about what I heard Joanna and Elliott arguing about before his death.

He doesn't say a word, but he nods, tapping his pen against his notepad. "Alright, Quinn. For now, you're free to go, but I may need to speak with you again. Please don't leave town without informing me."

"I'll be here through the funeral, at least."

"Alright. That's all I have for now. If you think of anything else, don't hesitate to contact me."

I let out a deep breath. "Will do."

I stand up and walk to the door to exit.

As I close the door behind me, I take a deep breath to calm myself down. That incident was more intense than I'd thought it would be. This isn't the first time I've been interviewed by the police personally or professionally, but this time is different.

"Quinn?"

A soft voice pulls me from my thoughts, and I look up to see Laura standing there, her eyes red and swollen from crying once again. Despite her obvious distress, she manages a weak smile as she approaches me.

"How did it go?"

"About as well as you can expect." I attempt to offer her some comfort through my own smile. Putting on a brave face for Laura is a struggle though. Despite feeling like I did well answering the sheriff's questions, I know that is only a small part of this. There is still a very real possibility of foul play in Elliott's death, and the additional factors of his affair and possible financial troubles. I can't put those things out of my head.

Laura wraps her arms around herself. "I'm so scared, Quinn," she whispers, her voice catching in her throat. "I don't know what to do about any of this."

"I'm not sure either if I'm being honest."

It's at that moment that a door down the hall swings open with a sudden bang, causing both Laura and me to jump. When I see the person fly down the hall, I call out her name.

"Joanna?"

She pauses for just a moment, her eyes shifting between Laura and me before she mutters something under her breath and hurries out the front door.

"Joanna!" I call again, taking a step toward her. But it's too late; she's already getting into her car and driving away.

"Quinn," Laura whispers, grabbing my arm and pulling me back toward her. "What's wrong with her?"

"I have no idea. Did you talk to her after I was in there with Sheriff Murray?"

"No. We didn't say a word to one another."

Before I can say another word, Laura and I watch as more police cars are driving down the driveway. We are forced to move out of the way as police officers make their way through the rooms, and Mrs. Fleming and the rest of the staff come into the foyer. Seeing the staff like this again is almost reminiscent of what happened when I arrived in Harrow Isle and Elliott brought me here for the first time.

Officers begin cordoning off areas while a few in plain clothes discuss matters with Mrs. Fleming and other staff members. It's a jarring sight.

Laura grips my arm tighter, her voice low. "What's going on, Quinn? Why are there more police here?"

I glance around, trying to find a familiar face among the sea of officers. "I don't know, but I intend to find out."

We approach one of the plainclothes officers who's speaking to Mrs. Fleming. He introduces himself as Deputy Dawson. It is then that I remember that he was one of the officers who came to the house when Mr. Gregory was arrested.

Laura waits for Mrs. Fleming and Deputy Dawson to stop speaking before she interrupts. "Why is there an increase in police presence at my home?"

He looks up, his eyes briefly meeting Laura's before they dart away as if to avoid giving anything away. "Just following protocol, Mrs. Bennett."

Mrs. Fleming, clearly flustered, wrings her hands together. "They're searching the estate, top to bottom. They have more questions."

"Searching for what exactly?" I ask.

Deputy Dawson hesitates for a split second. "Evidence," he finally says.

A chill runs down my spine. This doesn't sound like a natural death investigation anymore.

That doesn't stop Laura's questions, however. "Evidence of what, Deputy?"

He looks between the two of us, perhaps debating how much he should tell us. "Because of the autopsy's initial results, we have reason to believe there's more to Mr. Bennett's death than we initially thought. So we are here to do a more thorough examination of Mr. Bennett's office, among other places."

That matches what Dr. Samson said earlier, but all of this

activity is alarming. I glance at Laura, her face pale, eyes wide. "Are you officially saying it wasn't a natural death?"

Before Deputy Dawson can reply, Sheriff Murray steps out from one of the rooms, gesturing to the deputy. "You're needed in here," he says firmly.

Dawson gives us a last look, his lips pressed into a thin line, before following the sheriff. Laura and I exchange a glance, but my confusion still remains.

Laura takes a shaky breath, but her grip on my arm doesn't loosen. "Quinn, this is too much," she whispers, her eyes darting around, taking in the chaotic scene unfolding in her home. Officers with gloves are collecting items, some of which I can't imagine are related to Elliot's death, but I know that this happens all of the time because they are trying to be thorough.

I turn to Laura and say, "Hey, let's get out of this hall and go somewhere quieter, alright?"

She nods, her gaze settling on a picture hanging over the fireplace in the living room, a portrait of her and Elliott on their wedding day. They both looked so happy. And given what is going on right now, it seems almost cruel.

Finding our way to a less chaotic corner of the mansion, we sink into a couple of plush armchairs. Laura is fighting back tears. "I can't believe this is happening, Quinn. What if it wasn't a heart attack?"

I struggle to find the right words. "We don't know anything for sure yet. But we will."

Laura wipes her tears, taking a moment to compose herself. "What about Joanna leaving like that? Do you think she knows something? Why did she run out of here?"

"I have no idea," I admit. "But once things settle down, I'll try to talk to her."

Before we can continue our conversation, Mrs. Fleming approaches us. "Laura, they want to talk to you again," she says, gesturing toward Sheriff Murray's direction in the office.

Laura nods, rising from her seat with a newfound determination. "Sure. Let's get this over with."

I stand to the side and watch as Laura talks to Sheriff Murray, but I'm far enough away that I can't hear what is being said. The only thing that I can think is that we're all in over our heads. I don't have any idea how this will turn out.

After a long conversation with the sheriff, Laura finally approaches me, her face pale but determined. She gives me a small nod before she speaks. "Quinn, we need to move forward with Elliott's funeral. I know it's what he would have wanted."

I nod, understanding her urgency. "Of course. Whatever you need."

She gives me a grateful smile, but it doesn't quite reach her eyes. "Thank you. With everything happening, it's just... I need to know that he's at rest even if this investigation isn't wrapped up anytime soon."

"As long as the sheriff is on board with it, we'll make it happen."

30

QUINN

Four Days Later

The steady rain falls from the gray sky, casting a somber atmosphere over the funeral proceedings for Elliott Bennett. I stand among the sea of black-clothed figures, observing the hushed conversations that seem almost inaudible against the patter of the raindrops. The mourners gathered around Elliott's casket are an endless wave of dark umbrellas and solemn faces. It seems that despite the Bennetts not having the best reputation in this town, everyone is still willing to turn out and pay their respects.

"Quinn," Sheriff Murray says as he approaches me, his voice low.

"Hi, Sheriff," I reply, feeling the weight of his presence as a stark reminder of the ongoing investigation into Elliott's death. It's been days since his body was discovered and the investigation launched, yet the cause of death remains unknown.

"Has there been any progress?" I ask, trying to sound casual despite the tension coursing through me.

Sheriff Murray shifts uncomfortably, his eyes scanning the mourners before settling back on me. "Not at the moment. We're still awaiting the final autopsy report, but I assure you we're doing everything we can to find answers."

His words do little to comfort me, but I don't want him to know that. I nod in response, not trusting myself to speak.

"I also wanted to tell you that it's okay if you want to leave town now, but we might be in contact if we have any further questions."

That gives me a small glimmer of hope, but I still say nothing.

"Look, I know this is a difficult time for everyone involved, especially for Laura," he continues, his gaze shifting toward the grieving widow. Laura's head is held high, standing like a pillar of strength amid everything that is going on. "But I promise you, we won't rest until we get to the bottom of this."

"Thank you, Sheriff, I appreciate that, and I'm sure Laura does too."

"Take care, Quinn," Sheriff Murray says with a curt nod before walking away.

As I watch Sheriff Murray leave, my gaze is drawn to a figure standing on the outskirts of the mourners. Joanna stands alone, her expression unreadable as she observes the proceedings from afar.

I can't help but feel pity for her even though what she was doing was wrong. She's Laura's best friend—or at least she was before she started sleeping with Elliott. It's obvious that she cared about him. She lost someone she loved too.

I tear my gaze away from Joanna as I sense someone standing behind me. I turn and find Luke. I swear my heart skips a beat at the sight of him.

"Hey," he says as he steps closer to me.

"Hi," I reply, keeping my voice barely audible amid the murmurings of the crowd. His hand finds mine and once our fingers are intertwined, I sigh into his touch. With just him near, I feel calmer, even when the world is spinning out of control.

"Are you alright?" he asks, concern lacing his tone.

"Am I ever?" I reply with a wry smile, though my eyes betray what I'm really feeling.

He squeezes my hand in response, acknowledging the hell that surrounds me, especially in this town. We stand quietly next to one another until the burial proceedings are complete.

Once the burial is over, Laura and I get into a limousine and ride back to the Bennett mansion. Most of the ride is silent, both of us deciding that our thoughts are better kept to ourselves than shared with one another.

The Bennett estate looks even bigger than normal as the limousine somehow makes the turn down the narrow driveway. I can see cars lining the driveway and small groups of people in dark clothes talking among themselves on the mansion grounds.

When the limousine pulls up to a stop in front of her house, I watch as Laura's shoulders slump. Her voice breaks as she whispers, "I don't think I can do this, Quinn."

"We can do this together."

Our driver opens the door, and we step out of the vehicle. I turn my head to see Luke once again, and he's walking toward us.

Laura speaks first. "I didn't expect to see you here."

Luke's gaze is tender. "Elliott and I weren't friends, but I wouldn't wish this on anyone. And I wanted to be here for both of you."

Luke takes a step forward and gives Laura a hug that I don't think any of us were expecting.

After a moment, Luke turns to me, and our eyes lock. Without a word, he pulls me into a hug, and I relax against him. "How are you holding up?" he asks.

"Getting by, but I'm worried about Laura."

We pull apart and he gives my hand a reassuring squeeze. "She'll get better with time."

Together, the three of us walk toward the mansion and we are joined by a decent-sized crowd of mourners who still want to offer their condolences to Laura.

Hours pass and Luke stands with me as the funeral proceedings begin to wind down. Those who have come to pay their respects gather around Laura and I watch as they offer condolences. For the most part, she's keeping it together, but I can see the grief in her eyes. Despite what she is going through, she graciously accepts each hug and thanks everyone for coming.

"Thank you for your kind words," she tells Abigail Cook, her voice cracking with emotion. "Elliott meant so much to all of us."

Abigail makes sure to give me a small nod with a glint in her eye as she leaves the room.

As the last few mourners filter out of the room, I notice

Laura's shoulders sag ever so slightly, as if the weight of her loss and the burden of her search for answers are finally taking their toll on her. I can't help but admire her resilience, even in the face of such immense tragedy.

"You can do this," she whispers to herself, not realizing that I'm close enough to hear her.

I watch as she takes a deep breath, her eyes closed for just a moment before she opens them again and gives a sad smile.

"Quinn." I hear Luke's voice beside me, his tone gentle, reminding me that I am not alone.

The last of the mourners disappear down the long driveway, swallowed by the shadows cast by the towering oaks that line the path. I shiver involuntarily as a gust of wind whips through my hair and Luke tucks me into his body, trying to shield me from the cold.

"Hey," Luke says softly, "you okay?"

I force a smile. "Just tired, I guess. This whole day has been very long."

"Understandable," he replies, guiding me away from the door and into the dining room. The dim light from the chandelier above casts eerie shadows across the wooden floor, and I'm reminded of my creepy dinner in here with Elliott.

"You know, I feel like I owe it to Laura to stay here and help her find answers," I confess, my voice barely audible above the howling wind outside. "But at the same time, I need to get back home. I was supposed to have been home now for over a week."

Luke nods, his gaze steady and understanding. "It's a difficult situation, no doubt about it. But you also have to do what's best for you right now."

"That's something I would tell my clients."

"It's time to bestow your own wisdom on yourself."

"That's true," I say in return.

"If you really need to get away from it all, you could always move to Harrow Isle. We could use a good therapist here."

"Ha, ha, very funny," I reply, rolling my eyes playfully. But as our laughter fades, I can't help but entertain the idea, if only for a moment. "Honestly, though, I don't know if I could ever bring myself to live here permanently. Not after everything that's happened."

"Can't say I blame you."

We fall silent because what else is left to say? Without me being closer, chances are good that whatever this is going on between us is going to end as well.

His gaze holds mine, and I see the warmth in his eyes, like a flame flickering in the darkness. Slowly, he reaches out and tucks a stray lock of hair behind my ear, his touch soft and tender.

"Luke," I say as my heart pounds in my ears. "I don't know what to say."

"You don't have to say a word," he replies, closing the distance between us.

His arms encircle me, pulling me into a tight embrace before his kiss lands on my lips. This feels so right, but I also know it's at the wrong time. When I pull away, I rest my head against his chest, listening to the steady beat of his heart.

In this moment, everything else fades away. Grief. Uncertainty. Fear. All that remains is us.

31

QUINN

The next evening, I find myself in the dimly lit living room of the Bennett mansion, enjoying the temporary quiet that surrounds me. I sigh as I run my fingers through my damp hair. I thought about trying to blow-dry my hair, but that seemed like too much effort at the time. In the silence, the crackle of the logs in the fireplace becomes a soothing soundtrack for my thoughts.

"Quinn," Laura whispers, her voice barely audible above the crackling of the fire.

"I didn't know you were in here."

I whip around and see Laura standing in the doorway. "I didn't feel like sitting in the guest room any longer," I admit.

She nods as she hesitates for a moment before sinking down onto the sofa across from me, her fingers twisting in her lap.

"Thank you for staying with me for so long," she says. "I know I've said this before, but I really don't think I could've made it to this point without you."

"Of course," I reply softly, my own throat tightening with emotion. "It's the least I could do."

Her eyes meet mine, and I can see that we are bound together not only by our friendship but now by our shared grief. Though we've each experienced different losses at different times, there is a terrible familiarity in the pain that clings to us both.

"Sometimes I feel like I'm drowning," Laura confesses. "And, like, I don't know how to swim."

"Me too, even all these years later, but we'll find a way to stay afloat. Together."

"Thank you," she whispers. Underneath the sorrow, I can still see the woman I knew in college: kind, generous, and fiercely loyal, even in the face of unimaginable pain.

"But with that being said," Laura continues, "you can't stay here forever."

Her words are gentle, but I can feel the meaning and power behind them.

I take a deep breath and look around the living room. I know she's right; I have my own life waiting for me back in Seattle, my patients who rely on my guidance and support. But the thought of leaving Laura here alone amid all this, including the unanswered questions surrounding Elliott's death, still bothers me.

"Who will be there for you when I'm gone?" I ask. "I can't just abandon you."

"You're not abandoning me. You've already done so much!" Laura reaches out to take my hand. "You've been my rock through all of this, and I will never be able to thank you enough for that. But you need to go back to your life, to your patients who need you. You can't put everything on hold for me."

Her words sting, but they're true. My patients, the ones I've dedicated my life to helping, are now left without my support, and I feel the weight of that responsibility heavy on my chest.

"Okay. I'll go back to Seattle. But Laura, please promise me you'll call if you need anything—anything at all."

"Of course. I'll schedule the boat to come tomorrow morning," she replies, squeezing my hand tightly. "And I'll come visit you soon, I promise. It would do me some good to get away from this house for a while."

I rise from my seat, pulling Laura into a tight hug. "I'm going to hold you to it."

We hold on to each other, drawing strength and comfort. The silent understanding between us speaks volumes. Pulling back, Laura tries to lighten the mood. "You better not become a stranger. We aren't going to wait ten years to talk to one another again. We can spend the holidays together or something."

I chuckle, brushing away my tears. "Deal."

Laura gives my hand a light squeeze before she leaves the room and heads down the hall.

"Well, I guess I need to pack," I murmur to myself, forcing my legs to carry me toward the staircase.

Entering the guest room, I glance around at my belongings scattered across the antique dresser. Memories of the past several weeks flash before my eyes, each one a reminder of everything I've been through while I've been here on Harrow Isle.

I can't wait to get home, I think, as I fold my clothes and start placing them into one of my suitcases. My mind wanders back to the city and how I will be stepping back into normalcy very soon.

"Hey," Laura's voice interrupts me once more. "I wanted to give you something before you leave." She hands me a small, leather-bound journal, its pages worn and well-loved.

"Thank you, Laura," I say, touched by her gift. "This reminds me of the journal you kept in your office."

Laura smiles. "I knew you would find it behind the picture of us. I wrote some things in the first couple of pages, but I want you to read it when you're home."

"That I can do. I promise."

THE SALTY SEA air stings my nostrils as I stand at the edge of Harrow Isle's weathered dock, gazing out at the waters that surround us. The island has grown on me in such a short time, worming its way into my heart like ivy creeping up the sides of the Bennett mansion. My breathing slows, a final attempt to capture all the details of this place, the scent, the sounds, and its beauty.

"Your boat will be here soon," Luke reminds me, his eyes scanning the horizon for any sign of the vessel that will carry me back home.

I nod and swallow the lump that has formed in my throat. "I know, I know. Thank you for bringing me back here again."

"Wouldn't miss it for the world," he says.

"And neither would I."

I turn to look at Laura, who's come to see me off too. She's standing a little closer to the water, her figure silhouetted against the backdrop of the setting sun, her blonde hair gently ruffled by the island breeze.

Moving closer, I wrap my arms around her in a tight embrace. "Promise me you'll take care of yourself because you deserve all the happiness in the world."

Laura nods. "I promise."

Just then, the low horn of the approaching boat breaks our shared moment. The vessel that will take me away is here, bringing my time on Harrow Isle to an end.

Luke and I share a hug and a kiss before he places a comforting hand on my back, guiding me toward the docking area. "It's time to go."

I tell myself this won't be the last time I see them because, if there's one thing that this trip has proven, it is that life is too short.

The planks creak beneath my feet as I step onto the privately chartered boat. My heart aches with the bittersweet feeling of leaving behind a place that has become so much more than just an island to me.

"Quinn," Laura calls out from the dock, her eyes shimmering with unshed tears. "Remember what we promised each other."

"I will, and I promise to read the journal when I get home," I reply, my voice thick with emotion. As the boat's engine roars to life and begins to pull away, I wave and watch as they wave in return.

Their figures start to blur into the landscape, and that is when my first tears fall.

Inside the boat, I find a quiet corner and settle in, letting the rhythmic motion of the waves soothe me. I take out the journal Laura gifted me and let it rest on my lap. I'm tempted to open it, but I refrain, not wanting to break my promise. Instead, I run a finger over its worn leather cover, thinking about what she might have written in it.

With a heavy sigh, I resist the urge to open the journal and dive into its pages. The journey back to Seattle will be a long one, and there will be plenty of time to read it.

The sun has started its descent, painting the horizon with hues of oranges and purples. As Harrow Isle becomes nothing more than a memory on the horizon, I let the tranquility of the moment wash over me.

Closing my eyes, I let the memories play in my mind, whether it be the good, the bad, the heartwarming, or the heartbreaking. And I know that I left a piece of my heart on Harrow Isle.

32

QUINN

"Afternoon," Reese, my assistant, greets me as I pass her desk. Her smile is warm and inviting, and I return it.

"Good afternoon," I reply, my voice barely above a whisper. I unlock my office door and step inside, shutting it firmly behind me. The familiar scent of lavender calms my nerves momentarily, but the memory of the phone call claws its way back into my consciousness. I can't believe there might be a potential lead on my little sister's disappearance.

I take a deep breath and turn on my computer, my fingers hovering over the keys before finally bringing up my email inbox. As I scan through the endless list of unread messages, I try to focus on the mundane tasks ahead of me. But my thoughts keep returning to the phone call I got the day after I returned to Seattle.

"You're going to lose yourself in this," I mutter under my breath, my eyes locked on a message from one of my clients. "You need to stay focused on your work."

But the truth is, I've been losing myself for years. My

sister's disappearance left a gaping hole in my heart and in my life. No matter how hard I tried, I could never fill it and probably never will. I'd chosen my career as a therapist in an attempt to help others heal from their own traumas, but in doing so, I know that I've only buried my own deeper.

Soon, the letters in the email seem to blur together, and there is no way I am going to be able to concentrate. I throw my hands up in the air and grab my purse, digging to find my wallet. I snatch it out of my bag and open it, pulling the picture that I keep of her inside of it.

"Where are you?" I whisper, tears threatening to spill over.

The silence is deafening, a cruel reminder that answers may never come. But with the possibility of a lead in her disappearance, I know I can't give up. I won't give up.

With renewed determination, I put the picture back in my wallet. I grab a tissue and wipe away the unshed tears so that I can return to my computer and force myself to focus on my work.

I don't know how long I've been working, but the sudden knock on my door makes me whip my head in the direction of the sound.

"Quinn?" My assistant's voice is slightly muffled coming through the door. "There's someone here to see you."

"I didn't think I had another appointment."

Reese opens the door and says, "It's not a client, Quinn."

She steps aside to reveal Luke standing in my office doorway. His tall frame leans against the doorjamb, his arms crossed over his chest. Despite the weariness that tugs at the corners of his eyes, he offers me a small smile.

"Luke..." My heart thuds heavily in my chest as shock

washes over me. I stand up with a start and push my swivel chair out of the way so that I can get to him.

Reese gives me a smile as she walks away, and then my eyes settle on Luke.

"Hey, Quinn." He steps into the room, closing the door behind him.

My legs eat up the space between us and I lean into him to give him a hug and a kiss. "What are you doing here?"

"I wanted to see you," he responds simply. He looks around my office for a brief moment, taking in the neat stacks of paperwork, the art on the walls, and the small potted plants by the window. "Nice place you have here."

I chuckle softly. "It's just an office."

"To you, maybe." He smiles. "To me, it's a glimpse into the life you've built here in Seattle, a life I want to get to know better."

I can't help but grin because I want to explore more of that later. "How's Harrow Isle?"

"It's the same as ever, though it feels different without you."

"I've missed you."

Luke pulls me into a gentle embrace, his familiar scent enveloping me. "I've missed you too, Quinn. More than I thought possible."

Pulling away just enough to look up into his eyes, I ask, "How long are you in Seattle?"

"A few days," he says. "Thought I'd surprise you and see a bit of the city."

"Well," I reply, a teasing smile tugging at my lips, "if you're looking for a tour guide, I know someone."

"I was hoping you'd say that," Luke responds, his smile matching my own.

Glancing at the clock on my office wall, I realize that it's later than I thought. The sun has already started to set, casting a warm golden hue over the city skyline. "Speaking of which, are you hungry? There's a great place I know not too far from here."

Luke raises an eyebrow. "Lead the way, Ms. Pierce."

I pack my things up for the night, and together, Luke and I leave my office after wishing Reese a good evening. Luke and I walk side by side through the city. The comforting weight of his arm around my waist feels wonderful and it's something I definitely missed.

As we enter the restaurant, the smell of grilled seafood greets us. We are led to a booth near the back, where the light from the flickering candles dances back and forth on the table. As the evening unfolds, we catch each other up on what has happened over the last few days.

Despite the warmth of our conversation, I can't shake the nagging thoughts about Laura that linger at the edges of my mind. It has only been a few days since we've spoken, and I make a mental note to myself to call her either later tonight or tomorrow.

"Quinn, Are you okay?"

"Sorry," I murmur, forcing a smile onto my face. "It's nothing."

Luke accepted that answer and we went back to our light conversation.

I push the thoughts from my mind as we finish dinner and leave the restaurant. We make our way back to my office, where we both get in my car.

I turn to look at Luke before I start my car. "Are you staying at a hotel? And if so, do you want me to drop you back off there, or do you want to come home with me?" The words rush out of my mouth and a part of me is afraid of what his answer will be.

"I am staying at a hotel, but I do want to go home with you."

I refuse to fight my smile. "That was what I was hoping you'd say."

The ride home is quiet and quicker than usual because of the time; all that is left is the remnants of rush hour traffic at this hour.

As soon as we step inside my apartment, Luke's phone rings. He looks at the screen before he turns to me. "Quinn, I need to take this call. It's from the manager of Harbor's Edge."

"Yeah, no worries. I'll be here. You can step into my office. First door on the left."

Luke nods and walks into my office for privacy. I find myself wandering to the living room, idly glancing over my collection of books, when I spot the worn, leather-bound journal Laura had given me.

With a sigh, I pull it from the shelf, sinking down to sit on my couch. If I'm going to call her tomorrow, I need to get this done.

Carefully, I open the journal. The familiar, delicate script of Laura's handwriting fills the first couple of pages. I'm expecting notes on Harrow Isle's history or perhaps some personal anecdotes. But as I begin to read, it is something I'm not expecting.

Quinn,

Elliott's wandering attention and Joanna's attempts at replacing me were almost laughable. As if I could ever be overshadowed. With Joanna's affair with Elliott and her currently being on Sheriff Murray's short list as a suspect in Elliott's murder, karma has slapped her in the face. It serves her right.

I made sure I dug deep into a few of the chilling stories of Harrow Isle to draw inspiration from its unsolved mysteries to serve my purpose. They were the perfect foundation for my masterpiece.

As for Mr. Gregory, it's so sad how easily loyalty gets pushed aside when dollar signs are in the equation. I offered him so much money and he just couldn't resist. He should have thought twice before accepting a payment by someone anonymously for "kidnapping me."

Drawing you into all of this was particularly satisfying. You stopped talking to me after my wedding for no reason. Countless times I thought about texting you, but wondered why you didn't reach out first. After all I've done for you included being there for you when you needed it most. But you weren't there for me. Given your history, your dedication to uncovering the truth was both predictable and touching. I thought that you would do your best to find me, dead or alive, because of your sister. And I was right.

The confrontation with Elliott? That was something I hadn't expected. It was a momentary lapse in

*judgement, but one I would do again. It made all of
this more thrilling.*

 *Don't mistake anything in this letter as remorse.
Think of it as a glimpse into the mind of someone who
decided to rewrite her story when things didn't go the
way she planned. It's been the thrill of my life
watching you, always one step behind.*

 Until next time,

 Laura

My heart races, every beat echoing in my ears. The journal slips from my hands, landing with a thud on the floor. The weight of Laura's confessions blurs my vision. How did it all come to this? The kindhearted woman I had grown to care for, harboring such dark secrets.

Distantly, I hear the click of my office door. Luke's voice sounds concerned, "What's wrong?"

I look up at him, tears forming in my eyes. The happiness that was a result of our dinner date now seems like a lifetime ago.

"Where is she?" I demand, ignoring the tears that threaten to fall from my face. "Where is Laura now?"

Luke looks at me, his expression filled with confusion. "Last I heard, she said she needed a change of scenery. When Mrs. Fleming stopped me the other day at the grocery store, she said Laura was on some long vacation, trying to get away from everything."

I take a shaky breath because it feels as if the ground is shifting beneath my feet. "Luke, there's something you need to know..."

EPILOGUE
LAURA

As I stand on the balcony of my oceanfront villa, I close my eyes as the sun beats down on my face, washing me with a warmth I haven't felt in a long time. This island is far away from the memories of Harrow Isle, and I'm thrilled.

Was it all worth it? The drama, the manipulation, the heartbreak? Sometimes I wonder.

The aftermath of what I'd done is nothing short of spectacular. Quinn, relentless in her quest for truth, Joanna, with her world turned upside down, and Elliott, no longer walking this earth. I almost feel bad for them. Almost.

I've made sure that I will be well taken care of. I had no problem ensuring I had plenty of money to survive on. Because it was clear that Elliott was going to make us broke.

Yet, in these moments of solitude, an inkling of regret appears in my mind. Was my desire for attention, for power, worth the loneliness I now feel? Perhaps if I had chosen another path, if I had confronted my insecurities head-on instead of conceiving this plan of deception, maybe things might have been different. Then again, my feelings of loneliness on Harrow Isle were worse than the feelings I'm having now.

Still, there's a thrill in being the puppet master, in watching how a single decision can affect so many different people. I might be alone now, but watching my plan play out the way I intended, I feel truly alive.

Now, in the aftermath, I can't help but admire how cruel life can be. I might've escaped the confines of Harrow Isle physically, but mentally, I'm still trapped there due to the choices I made.

Every night, I dream of that night, of the cold cases that inspired me, of poisoning Elliott, and the trauma Quinn was forced to relive due to me. I wake up, the weight of my actions pressing down on me like a boulder, reminding me that I didn't necessarily win in the end.

Then again, I didn't lose either. As I drift off to sleep, I can't help but smile. For better or worse, I'll be remembered, not as a footnote, but as a headline. And that's all I've ever wanted.

$$\sim$$

THANK you so much for reading The Isle. I truly appreciate you taking the time to do so.

IF YOU WANT to read a bonus scene from this book, please click HERE.

.   .   .

It brings me a lot of joy to receive emails from readers and if you want to do so, please email bblackwoodbookss@ gmail.com. (Please note the two s.)

If you would like to check out my next book, it's called The Actress and will be available in 2023.

Please join my newsletter to find out the latest about my new releases, giveaways and more!

BLURB FOR THE ACTRESS

Serena Winter's star in Hollywood is bright, but something lurks in the shadows. A stalker with a relentless fixation on her knows no bounds. Their motivation is to do whatever it takes to get and keep her attention.

With no other options, Serena turns to Nick Donovan, a former Secret Service agent whose past isn't all rainbows and shine either.

What is their solution?

They want to lure the stalker out using Nina, a mysterious woman who shares an uncanny resemblance to Serena. But the more complicated things become, the more Serena has to sort through what is reality and what isn't, leaving her wondering who she can trust.

Because when it all boils down to it, all that glitters isn't gold.

~

The Actress is available for preorder now!

ABOUT THE AUTHOR

B. Blackwood has been reading and writing since she was a little girl. She lives on the East Coast of the United States with her family. The Isle is her first psychological thriller novel.

Newsletter
Facebook
Instagram
Amazon
Goodreads

ALSO BY B. BLACKWOOD

The Isle

The Actress

Made in the USA
Columbia, SC
22 September 2023

23240248R00145